SEECHERS

BEYOND THE MIRROR

Book One
First Edition

By

M.K. Williams
Natalie Kavanagh

First published by KDP in 2020

Written by M.K Williams and Natalie Kavanagh
Edited by Tim Marquitz
Artwork and book design by David Provolo
Based on the short film *Seechers* by Nat Films Ltd 2019

Luxon-Drake Publications
Kemp House
152-160 City Road
London EC1V 2NX
United Kingdom
www.luxon-drake.com
www.seechers.com

This is a work of fiction. Names, characters, places, incidents and dialogues are
products of the author's imagination or are used fictitiously. Any resemblance
to actual people, living or dead, events or locales is entirely coincidental.

ISBN-10: 1-99-996287-7
ISBN-13: 978-1-99-996287-6

For Judah. Follow your dreams. Anything's possible.

Edition One (2020)

Preface

"In 600 BC, Greek Philosopher, Anaximander, discovered our universe was born from a very powerful, blue luminescent substance that was pure and without limits.

He claimed the substance came from the subconscious world, Nihilo. A world that lies far beyond the walls of our reality. He knew this because it was a place he had visited, uncovering unimaginable wisdom.

He shared his remarkable knowledge in secret, with only a few of his most trusted students. He called them Seechers.

He revealed to them that a minute amount of the substance lay dormant inside the pineal gland of the human brain, with substantially more residing in the minds of those who are extremely imaginative.

On his death bed, he uttered that those who carry enough of the substance have the potential to unlock great power.

Over thousands of years, the Seechers advanced their knowledge and skills to manipulate reality by developing a way to carefully extract the blue substance from their own minds and contain it inside an object. A Seecher Key. The crux to a Seecher's power.

To this day, the Seechers work in secret, protecting their ancient knowledge from those who would otherwise abuse this power. Ensuring that the truth is forever guarded, they train new potential candidates, every seven years, through a series of mental and physical trials, to become the next generation of Seechers."

The Seecher Covenant

Awakenings

The large metal doors thrust open before Aris had even reached them. It was as though he'd willed them apart.

An unnerving determination glistened in his big blue eyes. His long, mousy-blonde hair brushed off his brow as he hit the outside air. His pace was so quick he barely managed to read the sign that indicated he was now on the roof. Not slowing for an instant, Aris bolted to the edge. Peering over and taking in the long drop, he knew the only way out was to jump. The building was thirteen-stories high. The only chance of survival was to land in the river below.

Panting hard, the cold air gave form to his breath. Aris had risked everything to be in the Curative Analytical building this night. Tightly held in his hand was a small, glass column-shaped hard drive. It glowed with a beautiful blue luminescence and was of a value he could barely comprehend. Yet he knew he had to escape with it. He had to keep it safe and, eventually, destroy it.

"STOP!" a loud, harsh female voice cut through the frosty air like a sledgehammer through a block of ice.

It wasn't the shrillness of the voice that immobilized Aris, it was the familiarity. He knew exactly who was behind him.

Slow and fearful, he twisted to face her. Memories of the recent dreams he'd had, of this exact moment on the roof, raced through his mind. He knew the dreams had been a glimpse into the future. That, one day, this horrible scene would unfold. He just hadn't foreseen how quickly it would transpire. Nor had he anticipated that the silhouette of the woman, who now stood in front of him, would become someone he'd grown to love.

The outline became clearer as she stepped into the moonlight. Even in the darkness of night, Aris could still make out her piercing eyes. Maya Green stood tall, glaring towards him. Her long blonde hair wisped in the breeze.

Aris took a large gulp of air before he uttered her name. "Maya." There was a tremble in his voice. He paused, not sure what else to say. He tried to remember what he'd said in the dreams.

"I can't believe this is *really* happening," Maya said, her voice shredding and her eyes filling with tears. She stood bold as she often did. Except, this time, held at arm's length was a handgun, that she pointed squarely at Aris.

"The others will be here soon. There's still time to make this right," Aris declared with confidence, though he lied.

"Aris, please, you have to give it back. This means more to me than it does to you!" Maya requested as she outstretched her left hand.

"I can't! How many others are going to die if this carries on?! I can't let this happen. I'm sorry, Maya." Aris edged back.

He could hear distant footsteps race up the stairs he'd not long sprinted up. He raised the glowing hard drive high in the air as the heel of his shoe touched the edge of the roof. He tentatively glanced over his shoulder and down at the river before turning his attention back to Maya.

Tears tumbled down Maya's face as her hand shook. She shouted loud enough so those rushing up the stairs could hear. "Give me the hard drive!"

Several men armed with guns hurried out of the doorway. She wiped her tears away before any of them reached her side.

"I forgive you," Aris said softly as he looked down again, mustering the courage to jump.

Maya was now flanked by security guards and, joining her was Dr Rivers. A tall man, with a large jaw and pitted skin.

"That hard drive's property of Curative Analytical. You're trespassing and stealing. I'm not sure what business you have here, or what you think you know about that drive, but if you come away from the edge now, we'll sit down and talk about it. We won't press any charges against you. Just come this way." Dr Rivers urged as he stretched out his hand and took one step closer.

"No!" Aris shouted.

"What are you going to do, boy? Jump?! Don't be a fool. You'll never survive that fall. Is this really worth risking your life over?" Dr Rivers reasoned, with a painfully fake smile.

A deep fear consumed Aris. This moment had unravelled eerily in exactly the same way he'd seen in his dreams. Except he knew the dreams always became fragmented and unclear from here on in.

"Step away from the edge. You're putting yourself in great danger," Dr Rivers shouted.

Aris turned and prepared to leap. But before he could, the sound of a gunshot rang out. He stumbled on the spot for a moment as an immense pain blasted through him. A bullet had pierced through his back and ripped out from his abdomen.

He cocked his head towards Maya and saw a plume of smoke empty from the barrel of her gun. Blood quickly saturated his clothes. Security guards galloped towards him. His mind blacked out, and he toppled headlong, plummeting to the river below.

One month before…

Aris Fletcher had tried to get up early that morning but failed. The night before, he'd stayed up late, reading his old textbooks by Professor Maxwell, to prepare for the first day of his new university.

Realizing his alarm had long since gone off, he paced around, trying to complete all his duties before he could be on his way. Rushing around the small, modest kitchen, Aris prepared scrambled eggs on toast for his father.

In the cramped front room adjacent to the kitchen, Peter Fletcher flippantly handled a pot of his medications, removing the ones he'd suddenly elected not to take. Aris walked into the room and gave the breakfast to his father, who grunted as he took the plate. Peter had an oxygen mask he had discarded without concern to the floor. Still hissing across the carpet, he had left the cylinder running.

"Dad, you need to remember to turn it off when you're not using it. The nurse worries you're overusing the oxygen. If she knew you were just wasting it…" Aris finished his complaint as he picked up the mask. He wrapped-up the tubing and closed the cylinder's valve.

Peter ignored his son's gripe as he tucked into his food. With mouthfuls of egg, he managed to give Aris more direction.

"Put the old one over there. I stubbed my toe on the one you left lying around yesterday," he wheezed.

"Sure, sorry." Aris took the old cylinder and placed it where his father asked.

Aris looked at the piles of paperwork on his dad's desk. He rolled his eyes before tidying up.

His father's cheeks reddened.

"Don't fuss, just leave it. I'll sort it out later. You don't want to be late for your first day!"

Aris looked at the time. He was cutting it fine.

"Are you sure you'll be okay?"

His dad barked back at him, "Of course. I'm fine. Go. Get out of here."

Aris snatched-up his bag and jacket, off a broken coat stand, in the narrow and dusty hallway.

"Call me if you need anything," Aris said with a soft sigh. He popped his head back into the front room to give his father one last glance before leaving the house.

"So, the question for today is not what *is* consciousness, but why is something conscious in the first place?"

Aris peered through a crack in the door as he watched Professor Maxwell press a button on his remote control. A conundrum appeared on the board. Aris was late and unsure whether to enter or not. But the professor had a serene presence and a charismatic smile, that encouraged Aris to just stay where he was, until he found the right moment to sneak into the lecture.

"When we look at this in the biological sense, what we're asking is, does consciousness come from a collection of areas in the brain all interacting with one another, or in a single part of the brain?" The professor moved on to his next slide, which showed an image of a human brain separated into areas, the pineal gland in deep bright blue, and all other areas in duller colours.

"Sir, when you say in a biological sense, what other ways are there to view and challenge consciousness?" said a wide-eyed boy in the front row.

"Well, Mr Matthews, consciousness as a concept is still very much up for debate. What constitutes consciousness? What level of self-aware-ness means something is conscious? What level of communication dic-tates something is conscious? We could also look at the origins of the concept. The criteria for definition. The varied definitions themselves. We could look at it from a religious point of view. A psychological view. Even from a linguistic perspective." Professor Maxwell turned to open a plastic box and took out a model of a brain.

Aris decided now was a good time and pushed the heavy door open. There was a loud *creak*.

Stood at the top of the theatre, Aris scanned the packed room, searching for an empty seat. He was totally unaware that the professor was speaking to him, until he noticed a sea of faces had turned to look up.

"I know the name of every single person in this class, and you, young sir, are unknown to me. Two questions. Who are you? And why do you think it acceptable to waltz in to a lecture, fifteen minutes late?"

"Sorry, Professor. I enrolled on campus yesterday and hadn't worked out my timetable. Sorry," Aris blushed a crimson red.

"Clearly. And?" the professor asked.

"And?" Aris echoed.

"Your name?"

"Aris, sir. Aris Fletcher."

"I can't have you just stand there like a lemon, Aris! You need to take a seat. There's an empty one there next to Miss Green," he said as he pointed to a vacant space.

Aris trudged over and sat, placing his bag down. He took out his notepad and pen. The long, blonde-haired girl next to him turned and smiled. He returned the smile and was instantly drawn in by her. Her deep, blue eyes stunned him and, in that instant, the embarrassment of his public humiliation disappeared.

"Hi, I'm Aris," he said.

"Hi." She smiled. Aris stared at her open-mouthed.

"I'm Maya." She put out her hand, and Aris quickly shook it.

"Since we've had a mini-interruption, perhaps now is the perfect moment to see if there's anyone who wants a go at answering the Beyond Question?" The professor said as he flicked his slides off. Then a series of numbers appeared on the screen. It was a long, abstract equation made up of many numbers and symbols.

"What's this?" Aris asked Maya.

"It's a question Pep's been running for ages. There's a Facebook group on it."

"Oh, right." He paused, "Pep?"

"Professor Maxwell. You can call him Pep. That's what everyone calls him."

"Right. And this question?"

"It's a tradition. The professor proposed it ages ago, and it's remained a mystery to this day." She opened her notes on the question.

"What?" Aris thought this a bit ridiculous.

"Yeah it's a real thing. See if you can figure it out."

"Is there a point to this?"

"The rewards, if you get it right."

"What rewards?" Aris asked as he leaned in, a little thrill rushing over him.

"An instant pass on all your exams for his modules and a place with the research associates, the PP Club," Maya said eagerly.

"PP Club?" Aris laughed. "What's that?"

"It's a small research group. I'm not sure where the PP comes from, it's what everyone calls it," Maya replied. Aris looked at her blankly, so she continued to explain.

"The associates get extra tuition with the professor and get to co-author papers with him. You get invited to special events and things. Only the top percent of the class are members."

"Sounds very cliquey and brown-nosey to me," Aris remarked.

"I'll make sure I let the rest of the club know your thoughts on it, Aris."

"Oh, shit! You're a member?!" Aris died a little inside.

"Does that bother you?" Maya glared back at him.

"No, no, not at all. That's kind of cool," he mumbled.

"Shush! Tim's gonna have a go." Tim clambered to his feet.

"I looked at the equation and calculated the obvious totals for both columns, and I suspect the middle symbol represents *over*. So, I worked out the sum, which gave me a number. I then used an algorithm to calculate a possible word, and I think the answer is *water*," Tim said, to which some sniggered.

"Interesting guess. It is a guess I haven't heard before, and I'm fascinated by your algorithm. Perhaps you can show it to me one day. Though, I must advise you it is…the *wrong* answer," Pep moved back to put up his slides.

Aris stared at the screen, trying to decipher the meaning before the slides returned. *An instant pass for this module's exams can't be a bad thing,* he thought.

As the class ended, students quickly filtered out of the room. Aris slowly packed his things up to purposefully obstruct Maya. He wanted to stall her as he plucked up the courage to carry on talking.

"I'm really sorry if I offended you." Maya raised a brow as Aris carried on. "Earlier, about the PP Club. I didn't mean to be rude."

"Oh, gosh, don't worry about it. It's nothing," Maya dismissed with a casual wave.

"Honestly, it sounds really good. Hey, since you seem to know a lot, perhaps you wouldn't mind giving me some reading advice?"

A cheeky smile crept over Maya's face. "Make sure you have a strong light, don't keep the book too close to your face…"

Aris wished he'd seen that coming. He chuckled. "I meant the reading list. There's a lot of books on it. Where's the best place for me to start?" Maya packed her stuff away.

"Phh, Sober's book, and Matthen's one. They're the nuts and bolts of this module."

"What about the first book the professor ever published?" Aris asked as Maya got up and gestured for him to move out.

"Nah. That's not on the course contents list. How on earth do you know about that?" Maya stopped for a moment, eyes narrowing.

"I looked it up whilst researching the professor. I can't find it anywhere."

"It's out of print. There's a copy of it in our library. It's not widely known, not compared to his other work, anyway. It's old and waffles on. I wouldn't waste your time reading it, not when you've got four weeks of catching up to do."

"Right. Thanks. Well, I've read all his other books. It's the only one I haven't. He just blows my mind. Hey, maybe we could chat about it over a drink?"

"Maybe. If you make it into the PP Club, perhaps." Maya grinned as she patted him on the back and made her way out of the lecture theatre.

Aris paused for a moment to admire her. *Maybe is good,* he thought.

Aris placed two cumbersome textbooks into his rucksack before picking up another stack of books. The book that rested on the top of the pile he carried, was Professor Pep's first publication. The one Maya had advised not to bother reading. When entering the library, Aris didn't intend to ignore Maya's advice. But when he stumbled across *Reflections of the Subconscious*, the professor's first ever published book on the shelf, he couldn't help but feel drawn to it.

Aris was amused that the book was so old, that it still had an old library check-out slip inside. Plus, it only had two date-stamps on it. A discussion with the librarian informed him this book was the only copy in their entire library, and it had only ever been borrowed three times before. Once last year, almost exactly a year to the day. The other two times were six years ago, and thirteen years ago, respectively. The most recent loan wasn't stamped on the inside slip as all the books in the library were now electronically checked in and out. *No wonder it went out of print,* Aris thought.

Walking with purpose towards one of the coffee shops on campus, Aris navigated past the many groupings of university students, all engrossed in their own lives. Overhearing tidbits of conversations, Aris tried to keep his head down. His books were balanced precariously in his arms, though his course was steady. That was until he heard an un-expected screech of his name.

"Aris, you fucking book-turd!" said a boisterous deep voice that bellowed from behind him.

Before Aris could turn, Leo Haile, a dark-haired, third-year medical student bounced on him and forced him into a playful headlock. Aris's books scattered to the floor. Leo ferociously rubbed Aris's head before releasing him. Both men looked at each other with beaming grins that stretched the width of their faces.

"You made it! How long you've been on campus? You were meant to text me the minute you got here!" Leo said as he helped pick up the books.

"Ahh, sorry. It's been a hectic morning. I was late for my first lecture. Got a lot to catch up on."

"How's your dad doing? I was really sorry to hear about all that. I friggin' love your dad and his toad-in-the-hole dinners," Leo gestured to Aris they take a seat on a bench, in the small concrete courtyard.

"Well-remembered." Aris was delighted to have a friend there to talk to.

The two men took seats on the wooden bench and continued to chat about his unexpected university transfer, despite being in the second year of his BA at Bristol. Aris had had to move back home to London to look after his dad over the summer, and when his father's condition worsened, Aris decided to make it a permanent move.

Peter needed a full-time-carer, and he simply couldn't afford one, so Aris volunteered to do it. Times had been hard for Aris, losing his mum not long after he finished his A-levels, which had resulted in him taking a year out. Now, his dad was ill, diagnosed with COPD and being pre-scribed oxygen, meant Aris had to move back in. The change didn't bother Aris too much. He wasn't really enjoying his course in Bristol, and being at UCL saw him being taught by several leading experts, including the renowned Professor Maxwell.

"Oh, shit, you were late for Pep's class? Damn." Leo said, winding Aris up.

"What's so bad about that?"

"It's hard enough to impress him. Plus, he really hates people being late. He'll never forget it. He doesn't forget a thing. That man's a machine mind."

"How come you know Professor Maxwell?" Aris asked. He knew Leo was studying medicine and was surprised he was aware of the professor.

"Oh, he takes some of our psychiatry lectures, he's a living genius."

"Oh right. I read most of his papers and books at Bristol. They're really hot on him over there. Hey, check this out. I got it from the library. It's his first ever published book. Have you read it?"

Aris showed the book to Leo.

"No. Not seen this. Phh, looks old. Someone in the PP Club's got to have read it," Leo said to Aris's surprise.

"Don't tell me you're in that PP Club, as well?" Aris whined.

"As well as *who*?" Leo lowered his tone and leaned in.

"Some girl I was talking to…blue eyes…" Aris's words and tone betrayed him.

"Maya then." Leo smirked.

"She seems interesting! She said we could go for a drink."

"Really?"

"Perhaps, well, maybe, if I get into the club," Aris mumbled as his gaze drifted toward the floor.

"Ha-ha. Good luck with that."

"What's that supposed to mean?" Aris slapped Leo's arm.

"Well, Maya's…you know, a bit untouchable. Guys find it hard to ask her out. She's known for giving the cold shoulder, is what I mean, and as for you getting into the PP Club, no offense but…"

"But what? I can get into some club if I want to!" Aris puffed out his chest.

"Pep's Club?! Possibly not, Aris. It's exclusive. Only the top four students from each of his classes are in it. To get in, you're gonna need to outscore four other very smart people who've probably been in the club for over a year and already have a massive head start on you, so…" Leo tried to break it to him gently.

"Not if I answer his equation question. That would get me in," Aris snapped back.

"That's the spirit, Aris. How's your maths?" Leo said, returning the slap.

"Alright, good point. I doubt I'll waste my time. It's stupid, right?" Aris exhaled. It was a small lie.

"Leo!" said another young man behind them.

"Stevo!" Leo replied as Stephen Monroe, a fellow medical student wandered over. Stephen was a round-faced intellect, who played rugby on the University's A team.

"Stephen, this is Aris. Aris, this is Stephen. He, too, is a member of the PP Club."

"Oh, for fuck's sake! Is everyone around here a member?!" Aris leapt up.

Stephen laughed and shook Aris's hand.

What the hell goes on in this bloody club? Aris thought.

Aris didn't mind being back in his old room. It was a humbling experience, but not a bad one. He took out his laptop and went through his diary. He wanted to plan his study time and lectures so he would be in the right place at the right time from now on. His dad wasn't in. Peter had already left for his support group for COPD patients. Aris was thankful for that group. It was his dad's only escape from the house, which meant Aris could get some time to himself.

An hour passed, and his diary was now full. Even dates and times to complete certain assignments had been added. Aris turned his attention to Pep's module pages on the university's website. Clicking through the course content, it didn't take long before he saw some links to different study groups. One Facebook group chat caught his attention: *Answering Pep's Big Question.*

Opening the link and joining the group, Aris was overwhelmed with the many posts from past and present students. As he scrolled down, he saw numerous guesses and theories on what the question actually was. Some suggestions alleged there was no answer to the question at all. Spending nearly half an hour scrolling through the page and reading thread after thread, Aris's heart skipped a beat as his eyes fell upon one post. A suggestion posted on the group by none other than, Maya Green.

Does anyone else think that the calculation is as basic as it seems and that the two numbers, which so many people keep dividing from one another, aren't just numbers, but are possibly coordinates?

As Aris read her post, he couldn't help but see her face in his mind's eye. He had only ever met her once but had thought of her several times since.

Her suggestion on the page was curious. Aris became intrigued with her thoughts and grabbed a pen and jotted down the two calculations previous students had already deciphered. 172149 and 284132 were the two answers from the complex equations that far more mathematically-minded students had answered.

Aris continued to read the thread and saw how many students had dismissed Maya's theory. Looking at the date, his jaw dropped when he realised this post was written over a year ago. Staring at her name on the screen, Aris was unaware the front door had opened; until his dad's voice croaked from downstairs.

"Aris. Aris… Move your God damn books off my table!"

Aris closed his computer screen and rushed down. He watched as his dad stumbled into one of the dining room chairs to grab the mask attached to the oxygen cylinder beside it. Peter pressed the mask against his mouth and turned the cylinder on. Moving the books to one side, Aris grabbed his dad's arm to steady him.

"I'm fine. Don't fuss. Just a little short of breath. It's walking up that bloody long path that finishes me off." His dad wheezed.

Aris watched his dad for a few more seconds, but didn't want to stare too much, before picking up his books and taking them upstairs. Entering his bedroom, the books found refuge on his bed. Professor Maxwell's book drew him in again, much like it did in the library earlier that day. Evening had settled over, and Aris needed to turn on his bedroom light so he could read the book.

He traced his finger over the front cover. It was an image of the planets in the solar system drenched in remarkable colours. All orbiting a crisp white illustration of the brain. Aris opened the book and examined the contents page. There was nothing revolutionary in any of the subject titles. The pages of the book were an off-white colour, and the texture had become hardened over time.

Aris enthusiastically skimmed through a few chapters, but it seemed Maya was right. It was an unnecessary read. However, just before giving up all together on the old book, he flicked back to the contents page. Sitting up straight, Aris's eyes fell upon a small, five-lined symbol at the bottom. It was familiar, but he couldn't recall where he'd seen it before. Touching the symbol, his fingertip felt it raised slightly on the page. On further inspection, Aris realised it had been drawn in by hand.

His phone rang loudly, making him leap out of his skin. It was Leo.

"Hey, where are you? We're at the Union." Aris pulled the phone from his ear and checked the time.

"Shit. Sorry. I'll leave now."

"Hurry up. You'll have to take a forfeit for being late. Them's the rules. Ha!"

Aris ended the call. He checked in on his dad, who was now snoozing in his armchair, before grabbing his jacket and leaving the house.

Leo wasn't lying. That night, Aris had to down two pints as soon as he arrived as a forfeit for being late. He didn't manage to down them, but he'd finished them both off within fifteen minutes of being there. It was the start of how the evening went.

Leo introduced Aris to all his med-student friends. Nights spent at the student union bar were always a filthy affair, and given the amount Aris had drunk by the end of it, he wouldn't remember much.

Stumbling out at one-thirty, Aris left Leo and Stephen behind as he made his way for the night bus. He was doing well to walk straight, and before Aris knew it, he could see the bus stop at the end of the road.

"Shush, not so loudly, there may still be people around at this hour," a soft voice carried through the air.

Aris immediately looked towards the open office window, where the voice had come from. Frowning, Aris strained to hear more. He knew that voice.

It was Professor Maxwell's.

Aris, as stealthy as a drunk person can, clambered over a low wall to get closer.

"I'll keep my voice down." Aris had never heard that voice before.

"That would be wise. Now … Three. And she … kidnapped … where … and the police … nothing. That's… better for us… We don't need to be… Our backs… Don't want anyone… Interfering … our affairs." Aris's mouth slowly dropped open as the professor's unnerving words faded in and out of his hearing.

"I know. Don't worry, Pep, they don't know anything. We're safe." The stranger's voice was louder.

"I don't … anything to go wrong. We have… sacrificed… much …anyone find out… Not now." The professor's voice became more intense. Aris started to stumble, and before he could stop himself, he fell forwards, landing awkwardly with a loud *thud*. The voices fell silent.

Aris quickly clambered back over the wall, running as fast as he could to the bus stop. He certainly didn't want to be caught eavesdropping on the professor. After all, he wasn't exactly sure what he'd heard. His heart raced as he questioned whether or not the drink was playing tricks on him. He kept going towards the bus stop. He didn't dare look back.

And as luck would have it, the night bus pulled up just in time to hop on.

———

The rain fell heavily onto Aris's face. Any other day it would have aggravated him deeply, but not today. Today, there was something refreshing and soothing as the droplets traced down his cheeks. He walked towards the university building. His head pounded, and his stomach panged.

He was sure this was the worst hangover he'd ever had.

A well-meaning student pushed a flyer into Aris's hand, shouting something about, "Healthy, non-smokers can give blood and do a psychometric test for cash at Curative Analytical."

Aris indecisively took the flyer and briefly mulled over it before crumpling it up into his pocket.

Pushing through the doors and entering the main building, it wasn't long before he navigated his way down the corridor and into an on-campus café. As he entered, the smell of coffee stimulated his senses, which was a mixed blessing for him. He desired caffeine deeply, but knew his stomach was far from ready to embrace the strong black elixir.

Aris's attention fell upon a group of students huddled around one of the tables. Sat there was Leo, Stephen, and the back of two heads he didn't recognize. In-between those two unknowns, was Maya.

He cursed. At the same time Leo clocked him and beckoned him over with a waving hand. Aris tentatively moved towards the group, hating the fact that his next meeting with Maya would be when he felt, and probably looked, terrible.

"I just gave some blood and did a psychometric test, in and out within a couple of hours. A lot of very personal questions, though." Stephen said to the group as Aris arrived and hovered near the table.

"And they gave you a thousand pounds for it?" said Thomas, who sat directly opposite Maya. Thomas Piper was a dark-haired philosophy student with a gothic look about him, which he accentuated with his choice in clothes.

"One thousand, three hundred. Came into my bank account this morning. Not bad for doing nothing," Stephen replied, the heavy night not appearing to have affected him at all.

"Who did you say this was with?" Maya leaned into the conversation for the first time.

"Some company called…Curative Analytical," Stephen answered.

"Seriously?!" Maya exclaimed, "That's where I have my internship!"

Aris scrunched his eyes, as he put two and three together and pulled the flyer out of his pocket to show them. "Was it this?" Aris passed the flyer on to Stephen.

"Yeah exactly that," Stephen remarked. Maya was quick to snatch it out of Stephen's hand.

"Yeah that's where I work," Maya confirmed.

"Oh, really. What do you do there, blue eyes?" Stephen said, blowing a kiss and moving closer to her.

"I process the psychometric data of poor dick-less students like you."

Maya snapped as she handed Aris back the flyer, smirking at Stephen.

"Ohh, burn, Stevo. Burn," Thomas jeered. Stephen glared at him.

Leo, Thomas and another student who Aris hadn't met before, Abi, all chuckled at Maya's insult.

Abi French had a soft, dark completion, braided hair, and a tuneful laugh, which was usually louder than everyone else's.

Aris giggled too, mostly because it was difficult not to laugh, when Abi did.

"Aris, you're looking rough this morning. Heavy night?" Leo teased.

"Don't you know it," Aris replied as he grabbed a chair and sat down to join them.

"Oh, sorry, me being rude. Abi, Thomas, Maya, this is my old primary school friend, Aris. He's just transferred from Bristol. He's also a philosophy student," Leo added.

"Yeah, we met yesterday," Maya acknowledged.

"I know who you are. You're the late guy from Pep's lecture," Thomas said pointing a finger at him.

"Great. Thanks for reminding me." Aris tried not to blush. "How do you all know each other?" Aris continued, attempting to move the conversation away from him.

"The PP Club," Abi said.

"Oh, for Christ's sakes, not more of you!" Aris remarked, but looking at their faces, he quickly realised this was *their* group, and he was out of place, not them. So, he tactfully changed course to a compliment. "So, you're the smartest guys in my class then?"

Abi, Thomas, and Maya cringed a little at Aris's question.

"Bingo," Thomas winked. Aris knew he'd said the wrong thing but didn't know what else to say.

"Guys, it's time to go. Wouldn't want to be late to Pep's lecture," Abi teased.

"Very funny," Aris muttered.

They got up, except Maya and Aris. Maya collected her books and papers. When she finally stood, Aris mirrored her. Maya noticed. Then, suddenly, the fire exit door unexpectedly flung open. A strong gust of wind filled the room and blew Maya's paperwork out of her notebook and onto the floor. Aris bent down and picked up the papers. He accidentally read some of the bold handwriting on them.

Seechers, do they exist? Who are the Seechers?

Maya wasted no time to snatch them out of Aris's hand, "That's not for you to read."

"Sorry, I was just trying to be helpful."

"Thank you. Aris Fletcher. Much appreciated," Maya said as she placed the sheets inside the old notebook. She hurried over to Thomas and Abi, and the three of them left without waiting for the others.

Aris stood there for a moment, eyes narrow, nose scrunched.

"Don't worry, Maya's hot and cold with everyone, but she's a whiz on a computer if you ever need a hacker!" Leo remarked.

Aris listened to Leo's words but didn't process them. His current thought was on one thing and one thing only: *Why did she remember my full name?*

Professor "Pep" Maxwell stood in front of yet another packed out lecture theatre. The subject of today's lesson: *Can we unlock the full potential of the mind?*

The whole room was engrossed by every word the lecturer had to say, all bar Aris. All he could do was glance over at Maya. *Why was she so protective over that sheet of paper? What does it mean? Seechers? Never heard of it. Who are the Seechers?*

Pep went through the content of his lecture meticulously, with such enthusiasm and passion that it wasn't long before he'd captured Aris's interest as well.

The professor had gotten to his routine signature segment of his lecture. He asked the audience if anyone wanted to have a go at the Beyond Question. Naturally, a few hands stretched high, all pleading to be given the chance. A lucky candidate claimed to have done even more complex maths on the equation and produced a numerical answer. Again, Pep took little pleasure in announcing the answer was incorrect.

As Aris watched the failed attempt unfold, his jaw dropped as his entire attention was taken over by a small symbol at the bottom of the

Beyond Question slide. It was in that instant Aris remembered where he'd seen it before. It was the same five-lined symbol that had been drawn into the contents page of Pep's first book.

Aris found it difficult to sit still for the rest of the lecture. Time seemed to drag on. He had to get home and examine the book for further clues. As soon as the lecture ended, Aris fled. He needed to review his copy of *Reflections of the Subconscious* right away.

Aris's dad was in the front room watching TV as Aris burst through the door. He shouted hello but didn't wait for a reply. Entering his room, he picked up the copy of Pep's old book and flipped it open to the contents page. He stared at the symbol. It was undeniably the same as the one that was on the Beyond Question slide.

Aris read over the contents, read through a couple of chapters he believed might hold some insight, but nothing. Opening his laptop and bringing up the question, Aris's eyes glazed at the equation. He spent the next two hours, with the help of Google, deciphering the mathematical equation and ensuring the two numbers he had previously seen were correct. He finally arrived at the same two numbers for himself. They were identical: 172149 and 284132.

Aris hadn't eaten since he'd got home. He'd spent nearly four hours working on the question. His dad shouted up some time ago, asking if he wanted toad-in-the-hole for dinner, but Aris replied he wasn't hungry. Now, Aris was famished, so he went downstairs.

His dad was asleep in the front room. An empty plate at his side, his oxygen mask loose. It had fallen partly off. Aris stopped and fixed the mask. He then got a pillow to prop up his dad's head and gently pulled a blanket over him.

Aris switched off the races on the TV and took the empty plate into the kitchen. He made a cup of tea and ate some toast, before washing the plates and pans, that were still lying around from his dad's messy cooking session. Returning to his room, Aris again flipped through the old book, looking for any reference to the numbers. But there were none.

Letting out a deep sigh, Aris tossed the book to one side and returned to his computer. He continued to search the Facebook group. It was the first time since he got home that he thought about Maya.

He scrolled back to the comment she'd posted on the group a year before, then he asked himself aloud, "What if the numbers are coordinates?" He wasn't thinking of them as map coordinates but rather in a Dewey Decimal Classification kind of way. With that thought, he wondered, *What if the numbers are there to locate something in the book?*

He fumbled to pick the book back up. Then wrote the first set of numbers down 172149 on a scrap piece of paper. He wrote them out again, deconstructing it slightly, thinking of them as reference points: 172. 149. Looking at that, Aris opened the book to page 172. The page was all about biology and life. Nothing leapt out. He pondered for a moment on 149 before changing it again to 14 and 9. He counted the fourteenth word in the text, but that coincidently proved not to be the right answer as it was *water*, an answer he already knew to be wrong, and there was no ninth letter there, either.

Aris then changed tact and went down the fourteenth line and worked across to the ninth word. Oddly enough, the ninth word was the start of a new sentence on that line. It simply read, *Amino Acids: The standard building blocks encoded in life.* Aris wrote that down on the scrap piece of paper. Something about that short sentence in the middle of the page, seemed odd and purposeful to Aris. He quickly wrote down the next number in a similar deconstructed adjusted manner: 284. 13. 2. It wasn't long before he was on page 284, running his finger down to the thirteenth line and moving it across to the second word. Again, it was the start of another short sentence. He wrote this sentence underneath the last.

DNA: The code of life.

He went back to refer to the original question, and with what he'd just written down, he had a new equation.

"The building blocks of life over the code of life," Aris whispered.

Aris spent the next few hours googling for possible clues to answer the equation he'd just stumbled upon. His gut instinct was that he had the right answer. It was now nearly three in the morning, though, and tiredness set in. The final equation he finished on was: there are twenty standard amino acids encoded by DNA, and there are four different nucleic acids that make up DNA. That produced the equation 20 over 4. He wrote down the answer: 5.

He frowned at the 5 for a long time. How could the Beyond Question have such an irrelevant answer? *What does five mean?* Aris threw the book across the room. "Stupid book," he muttered as he closed his laptop, pushed the rest of his paperwork to one side, and climbed into bed with a huff.

"Five! Five what?" Aris said as he rested his head on the pillow before switching off the bedside light.

A week later Aris found himself in another one of Professor Maxwell's lessons, the first one since he had reached his answer for the Beyond Question. Aris held his head in his hands as his thoughts overwhelmed him. Was his answer correct? It made sense at the time, but five is surely too simple an answer. Why was Maya so cagey with him in the cafe? What was a Seecher? Did he really hear the professor talk about kidnappings? Or was he just drunk and imagining things?

"You okay?" Maya asked as she perched beside him.

Aris straightened.

"Just tired."

"How many hours did you sleep?" Maya enquired as she got her books out of her bag. Aris held up four fingers. Maya gave him a knowing smile.

Thomas and Abi soon arrived and sat next to them.

Aris pulled himself together as he got his books out, along with his scrap piece of paper with his worked-out equations on it. At the bottom was his answer. The number 5, next to the strange symbol he'd found in Professor Maxwell's book and had noticed on the Beyond Question slide.

Pep arrived late for his lecture. Maya commented to Aris that the professor was sometimes late, but no one ever dared pick him up on it. The lecture proved interesting and, as per the previous ones, the Beyond Question was back on the screen. The professor again asked for volunteers but, unlike before, no one seemed forthcoming today.

For some reason, everyone had turned shy.

"Really, no one's going to give it a go?" Maya whispered.

"Why don't you?" Aris asked her.

"Just because I admire those brave enough to have a shot, doesn't mean I'm stupid enough to embarrass myself," Maya said bluntly.

Aris listened to her words, brave and stupid. He could be both of those things and unlike Maya, he had arrived at an answer. It could be wrong and incredibly inane, but it was at least an answer.

"I hear that fortune favours the brave," he uttered to Maya as he raised his arm confidently.

Maya rolled her eyes. "Oh, God, here we go," she muttered under her breath. Aris ignored her.

"Mr Fletcher, you're raised hand indicates you wish to enter this gauntlet. Is that correct?" Professor Maxwell enquired.

"Yes, sir." Aris put his arm down.

"Go for it!" Pep exclaimed as he rubbed his beard.

Aris rose to his feet.

"Well, I started off with the equation, and going by something I read…" Aris paused and looked down at Maya, "the two numbers are coordinates perhaps. I found two references, and from that, I got additional numbers that brought me to an answer…" Aris hesitated.

"And? Go on…" the professor encouraged. His face displayed a hint of anticipation.

"Five," Aris blurted out, "I think the answer's five."

The whole classroom, apart from Aris, Maya, and the professor, burst out laughing. It was a full five seconds of roaring laughter. Aris gritted his teeth and clenched his fists as beads of sweat started to form on his brow.

The room dimmed. Then, most unexpectedly, the lights flickered on and off in quick succession. The room fell silent. Then the lights went back to constant.

The professor's eyes were still fixed on Aris.

Abi whispered in Thomas's ear, "The lights."

Thomas nodded. "I know, how strange. And did you notice, five times?"

Abi shuddered. "Yeah, I counted that, too."

The strange hush in the room was only broken when the professor shouted, loudly and confidently, "Correct. Aris. Well, partly correct."

Every single student gasped as they turned to stare at Aris. Maya snatched-up his scrap piece of paper to inspect it. Aris barely noticed. He was frozen to the core, unable to even speak.

"Congratulations, Mr Fletcher. You have answered correctly, for the most part, anyway. There's more to it. A second part. But you've done enough to impress this extremely old and tenacious professor. So, for that, count yourself a member of my research associates."

"An honour, sir," Aris murmured as he slunk back into his seat.

"You'll get your pass for the exams, but *just* a pass, though. I suggest you still work hard and take them all the same. To get an automatic first in them, you'll need to complete the rest of the answer," the professor exclaimed.

"Well done! What the hell. That was nuts!" Maya gleamed. Aris turned and smiled at her. He pinched himself, fearing he might be asleep, but he wasn't.

"Damn it, I knew I was on to something!" Maya said as she read through his notes.

"I saw your post. It seemed right to me. You should believe in yourself a bit more."

"Well, you certainly believe in yourself. Have you got any idea how long this has been running, and you just rock up and answer it? That's amazing." Maya handed the scrap paper back.

"Thanks." Aris blushed.

"I should really say, welcome to the PP Club. Hey, maybe we could chat about it over a drink soon?" Maya smiled. "Coordinates of what?"

"Pep's first book."

———

The dream Stephen had was intense and realistic. He often slept incredibly deeply. Heavy dreaming was a trait many Potential Seechers experience and, for the most part, it was a blessing. But not for Stephen tonight.

The door to his dorm creaked open. The noise was so faint it didn't stir him. The hour was late, and everyone else in the building was also fast asleep. Two men slowly tiptoed towards his bed. They were dressed in dark suits and wore impressive, high-tech glasses, which displayed information on the interior of their lenses.

As a cloth pressed tightly against Stephen's mouth and nose, his eyes blinked open. He grabbed the stranger's arm and tried to peel it off. His body thrashed, but it was useless. Within moments, he'd lost all consciousness.

"He's under," said the stranger who drugged him. As he finished, more men walked into the room.

"You two, take him in. You clean the room. It all has to go." Dr Rivers uttered. He was tall, with a long, pale face. As he moved over to the bedside table, he picked up Stephen's mobile phone and handed it to another man.

"Send out the usual texts," Dr Rivers said, handing over a hand-written form from a file. He turned and watched his underlings carry out Stephen's motionless body on a stretcher.

"This one scored very high, didn't he?" asked the man who'd just taken the phone.

"He did. That's why I'm certain he's one of them. So, hopefully, we'll have enough to meet the order. We need a decent amount," Dr Rivers replied as he looked at the large collection of medical books, before departing.

The only two men, still in the dorm, quickly and methodically cleaned it out, packing up all of Stephen's belongings into bin liners.

The *ping* from Leo's phone was loud. It was a text notification from Stephen.

- Leo, you're my best friend and the only person I can tell this to. Things have become quite bad recently. I'm struggling to keep up with everything, and the stress has gotten to me. I've decided to take a break from uni and spend a month or two in a rehabilitation centre. The faculty know, but no one else does. I've got bipolar in the family, and I've had an episode. The

medical costs are covered by my parent's insurance. I was hoping you could just tell everyone I've gone to visit my brother for a few months. I don't want people to know. When I'm back on track, I'll drop you a message. Sorry to just text you like this but don't want to make a big deal of it. Don't worry about me. You know what to tell the others, right? You're the best. Stevo.

EYES OPEN

In the moonlight, the streets of Oxford were beautiful in every way. Aris's pace quickened as the sound of his pursuer's footsteps came closer. Aris couldn't recall the exact circumstances of how he'd ended up in Oxford. Nor why or by whom he was being chased. All he knew was a deep feeling of dread, compelled him to run.

Entering a long, narrow street of shops, Aris looked around for an exit. But he was trapped. Unsure how he'd gotten there, he stopped and glanced down at his clothes. He wore a skirt and blouse. He shook his head and turned to glance at his reflection in a shop window. He lurched back. The reflection wasn't his. He was in the body of a young woman, of a similar age.

"How?" he mouthed. The female reflection mirrored back at him.

Alarmed, he put his hands to his face and body to confirm it was real. Looking back at the reflection, to his horror, his pursuers were directly behind him. He turned to see two tall men, dressed in black suits and wearing technologically-enhanced glasses. Both pointed intricately-carved batons at him. Aris looked closer at the batons and could see mechanical parts and distinct ancient markings on them.

Two prongs shot out from one of the batons, striking Aris's upper arm. The crackle of electricity surged through his veins, and his arm felt as if it were on fire. He collapsed to the floor, writhing. A hand with a cloth moved over his mouth. He took a deep breath in but had no air to breathe. An instant later, Aris jerked forward and bolted upright in bed.

He frantically glanced around his room. Sweat pouring from his brow, panting hard.

"It was just a dream, just another stupid dream," he said aloud, wanting to reassure himself.

Aris slid out from under his cover and perched on the edge. His sheets were soaked with perspiration. As he took a few long breaths, he looked to his bedroom door. It was open. *I'm sure I closed that before I went to bed.*

Thirsty, Aris got up to fetch himself a glass of water. At the top of the stairs, he remembered there was an empty glass on his bedside table. As he re-entered his room, he shuddered as an eerie sensation surged through his body. *It felt like someone walked over my grave,* he thought.

Shaking it off, Aris grabbed the glass and headed back down the stairs. Filling the glass from the tap, Aris stared out of the window. He had turned on a small light, which illuminated the kitchen side space but little else. Glancing over his shoulder, Aris scanned the room. He didn't see anything, though he had the strangest feeling he was being watched.

He shook it off, downed the water, and refilled it. The sound of the door handle gently turning made him snap around, spilling his water. He watched as the kitchen door, which he had closed moments before, slowly drifted open. His eyes widened as his adrenaline set fire in his veins.

Then the door stopped moving.

Aris tiptoed over. He hesitated before examining the handle but found nothing suspicious. His face scrunched as he contemplated what could have happened. The door had just opened on its own, but there was no breeze nor draft to cause it. He looked up the stairs, then behind the door again. But there was nothing there. He resumed his search for a possible explanation when he leapt out of his skin. His father's voice bellowed down the stairs.

"Is that you?" He coughed, the sound echoed through the house. "Aris?"

"Yes, Dad, sorry. I'm just getting a glass of water."

"Well, be quick and keep the noise down. Some of us are trying to sleep," his dad wheezed before returning to bed.

"I will," Aris shouted back, still holding the door handle.

"This is the next case file. Head office wants the scores completed by today. You okay to work on them until they're done?" the large lady towered over Maya as she spoke, dropping a large file onto her desk.

"Can this get added to my reference?" Maya asked.

"I'll add it on myself. You keep up the good work, and I guarantee you a job here after you graduate," the lady replied without hesitation. Maya nodded in thanks.

Maya spent most of the day ploughing through streams of data. It was Saturday, and whilst she would have preferred to be relaxing or spending time with her friends, her deepest conviction was for her to be in the office, working for the company, Curative Analytical.

They were the leading organization in psychobiological augmentation, and because of their unique research and development, they were the number one player in the United Kingdom, and pretty much the world. Maya had worked there as an unpaid intern for six weeks during the summer holiday, and she jumped at the chance when they offered her a weekend internship program during term time, with the odd evening here and there.

Her motivations were clear. They had access to an extensive library, which specialized in psychological and neurological research. They had access to everything she needed to develop and expand her knowledge, to ensure she graduated top of her class. If Maya wasn't at university, she was at Curative Analytical, either working in the Data Analysis Department or in their library, doing her own research.

She finished plugging in the test scores. She didn't know who any of them belonged to, as the data was all anonymized. But she was smart enough to work out which scores were high, and even smarter to understand what those in head office looked for.

The tests were designed, she'd deduced, to identify individuals who were exceptionally creative, those highly imaginative, not just smart. She didn't know what the reason for identifying these individuals were, but she didn't care. She was given a task, and she completed it well. It gave her future security and consolidated her status as top dog in class.

It was nearing eight when she packed up her desk. No one else was left in the shared office. It was usually barren during the weekends, and the floor she worked on was guaranteed to be completely devoid of souls on Saturday night. Now finished, Maya made her way to the library and began her personal study.

Her real goal was never to just be the smartest in her class. To her, that was a means to an end. She needed to excel in class so she could be in the PP Club. Which was, in fact, another means to another end. Though this was something she kept firmly to herself; her own private research revealed her deepest intentions.

The library, like the rest of the building, was quiet and empty. Maya sat at one of the many grand tables that occupied the main atrium. Placing her bag down, she took out two books. One was her own notebook filled with scraps of paper, and the other was a much older notebook. The pages of the older book were well-weathered, and the inside clung tentatively to its spine.

The notebook was beyond precious to her. She had found it three years ago and, ever since, she'd opened it at least once a day. She'd never shown it to anyone, especially not her father. She sometimes felt bad about her deception, but any discussion about her mother always resulted in him shutting down and becoming defensive.

She opened her mother's notebook and considered for a moment how her mother would have been the same age Maya was now, when she first put an entry into these pages. Maya wondered what her mother would have been like and what kind of a student she would have been. The only thing Maya ever had, to discern anything about her mother, was inked right in front of her.

She had never been able to have a proper conversation with her father about her. She understood that discussing it caused him great pain and even though she had an unwavering desire to know more about who Monica Green was, Maya had long given up trying to engage with her dad about it.

She opened her notes to a page that stated, *Potential Seechers.* Beneath that was a list of names. Top of the list was *Professor Maxwell.* The names below his were a list of over fifteen other high-profile, well-respected individuals, ranging from other professors to celebrities and politicians.

Maya scribbled down some thoughts onto another page. The subject was: *Those with unique abilities who may be of interest to the Seechers.* She added a new name to that list: *Aris Fletcher.*

———

Aris walked into the lecture theatre, blasting David Bowie through his headphones. He manoeuvred past several people, all staring, trying to catch his eye to engage with him. He ignored them as he sat down, eyes to the floor.

"Morning, rock star!" Maya said as she slammed into the empty seat beside him, pulling out one of his headphones so he could hear her.

"Morning," Aris replied. "Rock star? That's a bit much coming from you, isn't it?"

"Look around, Aris. Everyone wants to know how you did it. So, come on, any thoughts on what five actually means?" Maya looked deep into his eyes.

"My guess is as good as yours. Five senses, five fingers, five toes, five major systems of the body. The number of humanity?"

"Hmmm. Anything else?" Maya pondered.

"No idea. You?" he shrugged.

Maya blew a small raspberry type sound, followed by, "Nothing."

Aris looked at her for a moment before Thomas and Abi plonked down beside them.

"Hey, Aris. Welcome to the PP Club!" Thomas shook Aris's hand.

"Me and Thomas have a little theory about you." Abi chuckled.

"Ohhh, a theory. I love theories," Maya grinned.

"What?" Aris asked, looking around and leaning in.

"That maybe you've got a sixth sense or something," Thomas told him.

"Yeah, some people were saying you got the answer too quickly. That you've only just joined the class and cracked it *way* too soon. The rumour is you're either related to the professor, or you're some sort of mystic psychic," Abi added with a probing smile.

Aris and Maya laughed.

"That's ridiculous. Why would anyone think that? I'm definitely not related to the professor." Aris's cheeks reddened at the thought.

Before Abi or Thomas could continue, Pep arrived, shuffling into the theatre. "Maybe not related, but you're not denying you've got psychic powers," Thomas said in a whisper before finishing with, "We'll chat later."

Aris jiggled on the edge of his seat, dying to reply, but it was clear the lecture was just about to start.

Pep congratulated Aris again as he began, then moved on to the subject of his lecture, which he delivered in his usual zealous manner. Though he addressed the whole room, there were occasional instances when his gaze fell on Aris. In those moments, Aris felt as though the professor spoke directly to him, as though the whole room was irrelevant and no one else was there. But more than that, it was like time itself stood still. However, when the professor turned his gaze away, that feeling completely disappeared.

Staring intently and listening to every word, Aris was enthralled by the professor's insights. He didn't think anything could turn his attention away, until a woman cried out.

"PETER!" the female voice echoed in Aris's ears. He jolted around to see where it had come from. None of the other students appeared to have heard anything. Everyone was still focus on the professor. Aris scanned the rows behind him for the source of the voice but couldn't see anything unusual. He turned back to look at the professor and, as he did, the voice shrilled out again.

"PETER!!"

On hearing the voice a second time, Aris was consumed by a feeling of familiarity. Not with the voice itself, but with the feeling that panged inside. He had experienced this consuming dread before. He suddenly remembered the day he took his biology A-level, when he sat in an exam hall and somehow just knew his mum had been given a cancer diagnosis. He felt it again, even more so, the day she died.

"Dad?" he whispered under his breath. Maya turned to look at him. "Are you okay?" she asked.

"My dad needs me!" Aris said as he briskly packed up his bag and awkwardly stood up in the middle of the lecture theatre.

He dashed for the exit. Everyone's eyes followed his movements, but the professor, who was known for calling out rudeness or abrupt acts, remained silent.

Pushing the door wide open, Aris reached for his phone. He rang his dad three times, but there was no answer. He then quickly selected another number and called.

"Mrs Potter, can you go and check on Dad? He's not answering his phone, and I'm really worried about him." He hung up barely hearing her say she would head over right away.

Aris made his way home as fast as possible. He arrived just as his father was being put into the back of an ambulance. He scrambled over to the paramedics.

"What's happened? Is he okay? Dad!" Aris shouted.

"He's had an exacerbation," replied a paramedic. "He's unconscious, and we've not been able to bring him around. His oxygen stats are low, and his breathing's abnormal. We're taking him to the hospital."

"What? I'm his son," Aris said as he put his hand to his mouth.

"Jump in," the paramedic told him.

Aris sucked in a deep breath, as he climbed into the back of the ambulance. He shuffled closer to his dad, who looked pale and grey. His chest rose and fell erratically.

"Dad, I'm here. Come on. Come back," Aris cried as he squeezed his dad's stony hand tightly. Tears rolled down Aris's face as he realised there was no response.

The ambulance pulled away. Aris put his forehead on his father's and closed his eyes, using all his determination to will his father back to consciousness.

After arriving at A&E, Aris's father was admitted and placed in the High Dependency Unit. Aris stayed with him for the rest of the day.

Later that evening, after more treatment, Peter regained consciousness and eventually stabilized. The doctor was amazed at his rapid improvement and told Aris, the plan was to keep Peter in HDU overnight, and he would be moved to the Respiratory Ward in the morning.

It was now ten-thirty at night. Aris had remained at his dad's bedside for most of the evening. His dad was asleep, with a nasal cannula attached, which delivered a low flow of oxygen. Although Aris knew this was a good sign, he hopelessly watched his father's chest in case it stopped moving. Aris twitched his nose as his stomach rumbled.

"Dad, do you want anything from the shop?" Aris whispered as he nudged his father awake. Peter shook his head and went back to sleep. Aris eventually stood up. He had been by his father's side for the last ten hours. He needed food.

The dull, artificial lights of the hospital illuminated the sterile corridor. The shop had closed long ago, and the only other source of nourishment was a very unexciting vending machine.

"Bloody hell, what's wrong with a bit of chocolate?" Aris exclaimed as his eyes scanned the machine's rows.

Fruit, baked snacks, Weight Watchers' treats, and granola bars were all that were available. Seeing that one of the granola bars had chocolate chips in it, the decision was made. *This will have to do.* Entering the code and inserting the coins, Aris soon bent down to collect his mundane treat. As he stood back up, his heart froze as he dropped the bar. Reflected in the vending machines' glass pane was Professor Maxwell. Swinging around, he gasped when he saw no one behind him. "What?" He snapped back to look at the vending machine, searching for the reflection of the professor again. But there was nothing.

Aris paused, putting his hand to his brow. He cast his eye up and down the corridor, but he was alone.

He bent down and picked up the bar, letting out a big yawn. *Must have been a trick of the mind*, he thought. It wasn't the first time he'd seen something that wasn't there, nor the first time he'd imagined something weird. Before heading towards the ward and back to his dad, Aris decided to sit on one of the seats next to the vending machine and have a little time to himself.

Aris opened the granola bar and took a couple of bites. He looked at his shoes. Thoughts of how he hated hospitals flooded his mind. Hospitals had brought him nothing but pain and torment. He couldn't hold back the invading memories of his mum's failed treatments. His heart fluttered as the grief consumed him again. He had these moments where the pain would hit him, and it would all feel so fresh and recent, despite it being three-years ago that she finally passed away.

"Don't look so glum, it's just a flapjack," Maya said as she perched next to him.

Aris jumped out of his skin. He wondered for the briefest of moments whether his mind was still playing tricks on him. But she was so close and vivid. Even if his eyes were lying; the soft, sweet smell of her perfume permeated his senses. *My eyes sometimes fool me, but I can trust my sense of smell.*

"It's a granola bar," Aris clarified.

"Oh."

"How come you're here? Why…" he stumbled on his words.

"I've come to see how you are, Aris. Leo told me about your dad. I was concerned."

"Thanks. Leo's studying for his anatomy exam tomorrow," Aris remembered.

"Yeah, well, I figured you could probably do with a friend, and I've finished all my work. So, here I am. Not to imply you've got no mates or anything." She too fumbled on her words.

"That's very sweet of you," he replied, offering her a bite.

"I'm fine, thanks," Maya nodded. "How's your dad doing?"

"He's stable now." Aris let out a sigh of relief.

"What happened? Do they know?" Maya leaned in.

"It was his emphysema. He's had an exacerbation and lost consciousness."

"Oh, my gosh. Leo said you were there."

Aris continued, "Yeah. He needed his oxygen and didn't get to it in time. He was probably too busy on his computer, gambling what little money he has on the horses and forgot to keep his oxygen close."

Maya frowned. "Ah come on, don't be too hard on him."

Aris looked at her as if to say he wasn't. "He stopped caring about himself a while ago. Well, ever since…" Aris mumbled, glancing at the floor.

"Since what?"

Aris gulped before answering.

"Since my mum died. It was just before I turned eighteen, straight after my A-level exams. He hasn't been the same since. He hardly talks to me. Well, he just sort of barks at me. He won't take care of himself and refuses help. He's given up basically."

"Ah, Aris. I'm really sorry. Losing a parent's never easy. I lost my mum, too, you know," Maya said softly as she leaned closer to him.

"Really? I didn't know that. What happened?" He looked up at her.

"She died when I was two. I don't have any memories of her. I never knew her. Losing your mum when you're eighteen must be a lot harder," Maya breathed out slowly.

"It's not any harder, it's just different. A different kind of pain, I guess. It's still your mum," Aris said, pulling his arm slowly around her shoulder.

"You're a strong person, Aris," Maya said with a warm smile.

"Not really." Aris looked back down.

"Bloody hell, considering you've got all of this going on and you *still* managed to smash the Beyond Question, in your first week of joining the uni, may I add! Come on, you may just be the *mystic* rock star most of the class think you are," she chirped.

"Ha. It was just lucky."

"There's no such thing as luck. Not in the way we think of it, anyway," Maya said, squirming in her seat. Aris took back his arm.

"I probably need to get back. Check that dad's okay,"

"Of course," Maya stood up.

"Thanks for coming to find me, Maya. It really means a lot," Aris also got to his feet.

"No problem," Maya whispered, finding his hand, she squeezed it gently before letting go.

The next day, Aris left his dad at the hospital and went to university. He wasn't sure when Peter would be home, but he didn't want to stay there and fuss. After all, Peter had all the care around him that he needed should anything else go wrong. Aris sat through two of the longest lectures of his life and thought to get back to hospital when he remembered it was finally time for his induction into the PP Club.

Locating the small lecture theatre Pep used for his club meetings was not at all obvious. Aris was a little lost until he turned a corridor and finally saw Maya, Abi and Thomas ahead.

Maya saw Aris and a wide smile crossed her face, one that, even at that distance, made Aris's stomach lurch. The three of them stopped and waited for him to catch up.

"Thanks, guys," he smiled as he neared.

"You're welcome. No one wants to walk into their first PP meeting on their own," Thomas mumbled, speaking from experience.

"Hey, where are the medics?" Abi asked.

"Stevo and Leo? Leo said he couldn't make it because he's got eight more exams this month he has to pass," Thomas reported. "But did you hear about Stevo? Apparently, he told Leo he's gone to go visit his brother."

Maya screwed up her face. "What? With exam's on? That's a bit weird," she blurted.

"Maybe his brother's sick or something?" Aris remarked. They shrugged it off, then nodded in agreement. "Must be. I can give him a ring later, see if everything's okay," Abi concurred.

"I tried him a bunch of times, but his phone's off." Thomas took out his phone to show them.

"Hmmm, I'm sure he's okay, if Leo knows where he is," Maya directed Aris to the subtly-panelled theatre door that, if you didn't know, would easily be mistaken as a wall.

The four of them entered the doorway that, at first, just looked like a small, pitch-black room. "Is this a joke?" Aris whispered.

"No, it's a secret theatre. The stage is the other side. See, look up there." Thomas pointed with his phone torch. Aris could soon make out small, steep steps, which took them up.

"Wow." Aris's jaw dropped once he made it to the top. He was now standing at the back of a stunning but tiny theatre. It was the décor that was most striking. Beautiful, old wooden panels, carved with patterns and symbols.

"How many people does this hold?" Aris asked.

"Not more than thirty," Maya replied.

Aris followed them down the tiered rows.

The front row was already filled. The four of them walked to the second row. It wasn't long after that Pep walked onto the stage from a side entrance.

"Evening. Apologies for my lateness. I had to take a call from the states. How have you all been?" Professor Maxwell bellowed as he threw his bag onto the table.

Replies came from the mix of twelve students present. The professor acknowledged their responses before taking out a large box. As soon it was in view, the students turned their attention to Aris, who's leg started to jitter.

"Don't look so panicked. It's just your welcome pack," Maya told him.

"Welcome pack?" he whispered back.

Professor Maxwell moved closer to Aris and gave him the box.

"Thanks," Aris mouthed.

"You're welcome. Your place here is well-earned. I hope you make the most of the opportunities," Pep returned to the front.

"So, who's read the chapters I recommended by Husserl, Brentano, and Nagal?" Pep asked.

There were mixed responses from the group, but it was clear to Aris everyone there had read at least one of the texts.

"Those chapters are in the books that are in your box. I wouldn't worry too much, but you should definitely read the chapters in there by Nagal, especially as you're going to meet him in a few weeks!" Pep exclaimed, light on his toes.

"Meet him?" Aris gasped.

"Indeed. Inside your box, you'll find the details on the talk-list diary. Try to attend as many as you can," Pep winked.

Aris carefully opened the box as the professor went on about the three philosophers' work. Inside was a hefty book, the one with the selected chapters Pep referred to. There was also a diary, a couple of smaller books, an assortment of shop loyalty cards, a few small mental puzzles, a pin that consisted of two interlinked letter Ps, and a research associates membership card, with his photo already included.

"University records," Maya whispered as Aris studied the membership card.

Pep continued talking about the upcoming lecture at Oxford by Nagal and how he expected them all to attend.

"How much does the talk cost?" Aris spoke softly.

"The professor covers it. You just pay for your travel and food," Maya replied.

"Right." Aris raised his eyebrows.

The PP Club members spent the next hour talking about consequentialism and noumenon. Aris didn't enter the conversation once. He had little knowledge or understanding of these topics. Maya, on the other hand, relished in it. Aris admired how much she knew and how eloquently she argued her points.

As the PP Club meeting ended, Pep took an extra moment to formally welcome Aris to the group before they all stood up to leave.

"Are you coming for a drink with us tonight?" Thomas asked Aris as they headed back down the steep steps, toward the exit.

"Thanks, but I need to check on my dad, in hospital."

"Yeah, Maya told us. I hope he's okay," Abi said.

"Thanks. He's being well looked after." Aris nodded.

Peter was asleep. A book rested on his lap, and a glass of water was on the bedside table. Next to the water were his many medicine pots with a few meds still left in them. It didn't take Aris long to notice the medicine still left in the pots should have been taken hours ago.

"Dad, dad, wake up," Aris gently shook him awake.

Peter stirred and smiled as he saw his son.

"Dad, you haven't taken your meds? These should have been taken at six thirty, it says," Aris inspected the pots.

"I told the nurse I'll take them in a bit," was the sleepy muffled reply.

"No. Take them now," Aris demanded.

"I'll take them in a minute. Stop fussing."

"Dad. Stop putting it off and just take them."

"They make me feel sick. I hate taking them. Okay." Peter pleaded.

"You have to take them. They're helping you with your breathing. They're keeping you alive! A little bit of nausea is the price you'll have to pay," Aris's cheeks reddened.

A nurse popped her head around the sectioned-off curtain. "Is everything okay? We have patients sleeping," she said gently as she entered.

"He won't take his medication," Aris quibbled.

"Still?! Now, Peter, you promised me by eight o'clock, at the latest," she looked at her watch.

"Fine." Peter picked up the medications and threw them in his mouth, washing them down with water. As soon as he did, the nurse took the glass of water and the empty pots, then disappeared round the curtain again. A deflated Peter grumbled.

"What's the point, if I just keep vomiting them back up?"

"Dad, just do as you're told."

"You're just like your mother, you know? She was stubborn to the core. Always fussing over me, even when I didn't want her to. God, I miss her. She had such soft delicate hands. Do you remember her hands?" Peter reminisced about his wife.

"Dad, the hospital isn't the best place to remember mum."

"We have to talk about her at some point. It's like you don't want to remember her at all."

"Yes, I remember how soft her hands were." Aris put his hand on his dad's arm to assure him.

"We need to talk about her, we need to remember, it's good for us to share memories, you know before," Peter mumbled, but at the same time, he was starting to drift back to sleep.

"You need to rest," Aris said as he wiped away a tear.

"There's so much you need to know about her," Peter continued, drifting off.

"I'll come by and see you again tomorrow. You need to sleep," Aris whispered.

"She would always be fussing over me. Always fussing." Peter's eyes closed, and he was soon snoring.

Aris moved away and headed back out of the curtain. He kept walking out of the ward. Then out of the building.

Aris entered the SU bar and watched his new friends from a distance as he bought a beer.

Maya, Thomas and Abi drank in a booth, playing their last round of a heated board game. Settlers of Catan. They were tucked away, hidden in a dark corner, just the way they liked it.

"I have wood and I need brick," Thomas requested.

Maya swapped cards with him. Thomas slapped down another piece of road.

"That makes mine the longest," Thomas declared. "And with that—"

"Oh no, you shouldn't have swapped Maya! No. I'm so close!" Abi put her head on the table.

"Count it up. I've won!" Thomas exclaimed.

Maya methodically counted up his points.

"Damn! How could I be so stupid!" Maya clenched her jaw as she stared at Thomas's wide grin.

Aris joined them.

"Hey, Aris. You're here!" Maya proclaimed.

"Dad fell asleep. I'm not a fan of hospitals. I hoped you'd still be here," Aris said as he plonked himself down. "What are you playing?" Aris asked scrunching up his face.

"Catan. Amazing timing! Thomas just won," Abi scrunched her brow.

"Congratulations." Aris raised his glass.

"Cheers!" Thomas toasted.

"Does that happen to you a lot?" Abi leaned into Aris.

"What?" Aris said, taking a sip of his beer.

"You know that you just turn up at the right time, right place?" Abi continued.

Aris shrugged it off, Maya butted in.

"Oh no, not all this Aris is a mystic psychic stuff again. You know it's all rubbish, right?"

Thomas put his hand up to Maya. "There's only one way to settle it."

Abi laughed. "What you mean, like a test?"

Thomas nodded and handed Aris the dice.

"All you have to do is guess what number you're going to roll, then roll."

They all laughed.

"Sure." Aris put his beer down and took the dice. He shook them vigorously, then blew on them, then shook them some more. Maya sat back to watch.

"Come on then, call it," Abi insisted.

"Seven," Aris shouted as he let the dice roll. A moment of still, then a gasp. Four and three.

"I told you! He's psychic. That's how he got the Beyond Question right," Thomas remarked, directed at Abi.

"It's just luck," Aris shrugged. Maya rolled her eyes.

"A lot of people think you've got a sixth sense," Thomas came clean. "You've just proved it."

"That's not proof. Why don't you ask me about my dreams? Now, *they're* really weird," Aris gulped down his beer.

"Really? Me too. Do you ever get those dreams that feel completely real?" Thomas asked.

"All the time," Aris continued.

He went on to describe his recent dream of being a woman who was kidnapped. Then Thomas described one of his own dreams that was peculiarly similar to Aris's dream. He, too, had been attacked by strange men. Thomas described the dream in oddly-comparable detail. The cloth. The men in suits with technological glasses. These were all too specific to just be mere coincidence. They were almost identical, except Thomas was another man, asleep in a bed. *A dorm,* he thought.

They continued to drink and chat for a few more hours. Abi was the first to head off, followed by Thomas. One in the morning rolled around, and Maya and Aris were still there. Just the two of them.

"Can I ask you something?" Maya asked. Aris's heart skipped a beat.

"Go on," he urged.

"What made you think to go through that old book of Pep's? I know you got the idea from my post, that the answer to the equations were coordinates and not simply numbers, but how did you know it was related to his book?"

Pausing before replying, Aris's thoughts went back to the night he cracked the code.

"The same symbol on the slide was drawn into that copy of the book. I just recognised it. Hey, maybe Thomas and Abi are right and *I am psychic*? I mean, why did I ever pick up the book?" Aris's eyes glistened.

"I want to show you something. I've not shown it to anyone before, but I think you can help. In fact, it could help us both." Maya took a deep breath. Aris gave her a nod.

"It's this book, the one that the page escaped from. You remember in the cafe?" Maya took out the book and placed it on the table.

"You want to show me this book?" Aris tapped on it.

"It was my mother's."

"Go on,"

"This picture," Maya opened the book and took out a small picture of a young women who had a remarkable resemblance to Maya, "it's all I have to know what she even looked like. This book are her thoughts and ideas. She wrote it when she was roughly the same age as we are now."

"Wow, that's amazing. You look so much like her!" Aris said, looking at the photo, and then at her.

"My mum was smart. This book proves it. From it, I've learnt she studied at Cambridge and she was wise, way beyond her years. She was involved in something. I've spent the last three years trying to find out more about it, but I can't find anything else ever written about it. Anywhere. It's really frustrating. I don't think she just made it up. But I need to find out what it all means. If it's really true. And I think you can help me," Maya said, her voice dropping to a whisper.

"How can I help?" Aris blinked as he picked up his drink.

"It has a lot in here about philosophy, her life, her friends. It even has a record of how she met my dad. But more importantly, there's something in here I've become obsessed with." Maya paused briefly. "You know that sheet you saw? I know you read it."

"Seechers, do they exist? What are the Seechers?" Aris cocked his head.

"Yes, that's it. The Seechers," Maya replied.

"So, you're obsessed with Seechers. What is it? It's not something

I've heard of. Should I know something about it?" Aris gestured with his hands.

"Well, I've never heard of them, except in here. And my mum didn't start writing about it for a while, not until she got to Cambridge. Not until she started a certain class with a certain lecturer." Maya flicked through the pages.

"Professor Maxwell," Aris whispered.

"Exactly!" Maya exclaimed.

"There's definitely something very strange about him. I'm not related to him, but I keep…sensing him. Now and again, like he's there, but he's not. If that makes sense," Aris confessed.

"Yes, it does." Maya opened to a page covered in scribbles.

"Here, my mum penned her ideas of what she thought the Seechers were about. From what I can tell, they're some kind of secret organization, one that has existed since the ancient Greeks. My mum suggests in here, that they have had some amazing members throughout history. Descartes, Husserl, Da Vinci, Darwin, Einstein. She suggests it's an organization that stretches the globe and includes many very important people."

"Impressive. So, why haven't we heard of Seechers before? Like, what are they supposed to do?" Aris asked, swirling his beer.

"Well, that's where it gets vague. There's stuff in here about The Great Mystery. I suspect my mum was asking the same thing, the mystery being, what do they do?"

"Like this," Aris said as his eyes fell on an entry. "What are Seechers? What do they do? They are the keepers of the ancient truth, the protectors of the sacred knowledge. They are secretive and powerful, keeping a balance few can see." Aris paused, pressing his lips together tightly.

"Continue reading."

"The feeling that you've been somewhere before, that sensation you get when someone walks over your grave, the instinct of just knowing something, having dreams that mirror reality, an insight into something that just comes to you, even the feeling you get when you meet someone who you've never met before, but somehow you know things about them you couldn't possibly know, like you've known them for years. All these things, this is Seechers." Aris stopped and frowned.

"I know, it's fucked-up, right?"

"That stuff happens to me all the time. But I've got nothing to do with Seechers. So, it just happens to everyone. Right? It's just a part of life."

"Or is it? Perhaps there's something else going on? That we can't see. Can you explain how you guessed the dice roll earlier?"

"Of course not. But that doesn't mean someone or something else is responsible. How would that even work? It's just random chance."

"I don't know. I can't explain it, either. Hence my obsession with this."

"Does anything in there point to, I don't know, any other answers?"

Maya took the book straight back and begin to flip through it.

"Funny you should ask that." As Maya finished, she placed the book back in front of Aris.

The two pages were covered in hand-drawn scribbles. Symbols and shapes, pentagons, dodecahedrons, Greek letters and numbers. A fish. Aris struggled to see any relevance to any of it.

"They're just doodles, Maya."

"I thought the same, but this…" Maya pointed to the top corner of the second page. Her finger hit a circle, with several arrows pointing at it. Within that circle was the number five.

"Five," Aris whispered.

"You see, I thought this page was just my mum's brain doodles, too, but when you cracked Pep's code, this page took on a whole new meaning. I've studied it every night since."

"Really? So, what have you deciphered?" Aris asked, smiling.

"Nothing concrete, that's why I'm sharing it with the psychic genius who cracked the code. I need to find out more about the Seechers. I want to know if my mum was involved with them and what they meant to her. But all I have to go on is just this," Maya whispered.

"I get it. So, let's have a look." Aris pulled himself together as he drew the book nearer.

"The only thing I've managed to work on are those words in that pentagon. They're ancient Greek," Maya pointed at them. "That one means *life*, that one means *space*, *time*, *matter*, and that one's *mind*."

"Cool. What does it mean?" Aris asked.

"I don't know, but it means something to the Seechers. And, it's a five-sided shape. And these are surely the five things that answer the rest of the Beyond Question," Maya replied, looking at Aris.

"Probably. But what are we supposed to do about it? Confront Professor Maxwell? I can just ask him," Aris proposed.

"Well, I highly suspect he *is one*. And if this is a secret group he's in, he's not gonna just come out and say it, is he?" Maya sighed.

"Right," Aris said, a smile creeping back onto his face.

Maya continued, "It could be a coincidence that he taught my mum, but I can't risk just asking him outright and looking like an idiot. I need more evidence before I try and do that. But you...it's different."

"It's an amazing coincidence that he now teaches..." Aris paused. His smile faded as his eyes became like small beads. "You came here for him, didn't you? Don't tell me you only studied philosophy to be in his class? And the PP Club. You're only in it to spy on Pep? Just so you can find out about this?"

"I needed to know, Aris."

"Look, Maya, I'll help you, but you have to be honest with me. Every step of the way, you need to tell me. Obsessions are good motivators, but you shouldn't let them take over your life."

Maya promptly stood up and went to put her coat on.

"If you're going to be like that, I'll continue on my own." Maya took the book and put it back in her bag.

"Maya, don't. I just mean, you can become too transfixed on something to a point where it's not healthy," Aris said, standing up, putting his coat on too.

"Good night, Aris," Maya promptly stormed out.

Aris sighed. He needed more information, and like Maya, his judgment might be a little clouded, mainly from the beers he'd drunk. A reckless and inescapable desire to search for answers at that moment pervaded his mind.

Although the alcohol continued to surge through his veins, Aris thought he would just take matters into his own hands. He didn't mean to upset Maya, and he wanted to be able to say to her that he did something. Walking into the empty university, he still felt this course of action was the right one. He was on his way to see Professor Maxwell. Something inside, apart from the drink, compelled him. Aris paced down the corridor until he was at the lecture theatre where the PP Club had convened earlier. Entering the little, pitch-black room, he could sense Pep's presence in the theatre beyond. He couldn't see the steep steps in the darkness and didn't want to make too much noise, so he took out his phone to use the torch. But it was dead.

A few seconds later, he heard two sets of footsteps. Via the stage door, Aris guessed. He figured his best bet was to just stay put and listen.

"Are we alone?" a deeper voice questioned. It was the same voice he'd heard talking to Pep at the window. Aris stood still as his heart thumped in his chest.

"One second," uttered Pep. The sound of his chair moved back. The doors next to Aris suddenly slammed shut and locked by themselves. Aris's jaw dropped. He leant his back against a wall.

"We're alone," Pep confirmed, the sound of his chair squeaked again.

Aris slowly lowered himself to the floor, looking to the light of the theatre above him, trying not to make a sound.

"So, what have you found?" Pep asked.

"I haven't managed to locate your student, Stephen Monroe. I've monitored his family. They're unaware he's missing from university. Though he may well have been taken, too, I don't want to cause them any unnecessary panic until we know for sure," the man responded.

"If this is true, Pep, and we consider how many we've lost, this is extremely serious, and by no means do we deem this last case *a coincidence*. We've very little choice but to break the cycle," a lady said. Aris did not recognise her voice, but it was soft and caring.

"We're only permitted to break the cycle in times of war, Tallia," the other man replied.

"Potentials are being kidnapped, Adam! By an unknown agency! If that's not a declaration of war, I don't know what is," Tallia snapped.

"Please, both of you, calm down. I'll meet with the other Guild

Elders and take this matter up with them." Pep reassured.

"Perhaps breaking the cycle and making them Seechers isn't such a bad idea, then. If one thing's clear, we can't protect them all, all of the time," Adam concurred.

"It will be up to the Council of Elders to decide. But, in the meantime, we can at least ensure all Potentials are tested and begin to ready them for the activation ceremony, should it come to that. We can, at least, prepare. How many do you have for testing, Tallia?" Pep asked.

Aris's eyes widened as he raised his hands to his mouth.

"There are five in my group. Kat has six in hers. And your group, Pep?" Tallia retorted.

"Possibly four," Pep replied.

"And what about that new student? The one who cracked your code? Aris, isn't it?" Adam asked.

Aris now had both hands in front of his mouth and controlled his breathing to keep himself as still and quiet as possible.

"I've watched him and reviewed his records. He's on my list to test," Pep admitted.

"I need to get going, I have to be back at Oxford tonight, let me know once you've reached a decision," Tallia asserted.

Two sets of footsteps left the room. Aris remained frozen on the spot in the darkness. He wondered what he was going to do. He heard Pep's chair *squeak* again, then there was a brief *click* as the lock on the doors nearest Aris released. It was at this point he felt the courage to move. He quietly snuck up the steep steps, his eyes now adjusted to the darkness. With just the top of his head popping up, he could see Pep pack up his things and make his way for the side door.

Aris couldn't explain it, as he wasn't the most courageous person, but instead of moving back down the steps and out of the theatre, he felt compelled to follow the professor.

Aris tiptoed down the main theatre, onto the stage, and turned the handle to the side door. He held it gently open and peered through. He watched as he saw the professor walk down a long, dark corridor. As Pep turned the corner, Aris moved out of the room and quietly went after him. As he reached the corner, he paused and looked around.

He watched the professor tap his pass onto the security panel that opened the automatic doors. The professor turned and entered a stairway, which led down to the left. Aris moved as quickly as his legs could silently carry him. As he neared the doors, he could see them closing. He hastily slid through. The doors closed inches from his hip.

Creeping down the stairs, he could hear distant footsteps he assumed were Pep's. He heard another *beep*, which he guessed came from another pass-operated door. As he reached the bottom of the stairway, he could see a small corridor ahead with only one door at the end.

Approaching the door, he noticed a card panel on the side. But it was locked. He tried to open it, but the handle didn't move. What Aris couldn't see was that, on the other side of this door, was a small box that displayed a countdown. It counted backwards and was currently on nine.

Aris looked around to see if he could open it any other way, or if there was some other way in. But there wasn't. As eight seconds passed, the door beeped open. Aris turned to look at the open door. An eerie sensation prickled up his spine as he stepped into the next room. It was very small, with no other exits apart from the one he'd just entered. It was also completely empty, except for one strange feature. Large mirrors covered the whole room.

Impossible, Aris thought. The professor wasn't there. Aris searched for a secret way out, but there wasn't one. He stared at his own reflection and wondered, *How did Pep get out of here?*

Aris turned to look back down the corridor. He couldn't see anything. *Where did Pep go? He entered this room, so where could he possibly be now? This must have something to do with the Seechers, but what?*

Aris's heart pounded harder than it ever had before.

UNDER THE WAVES

Three tall men, dressed in smart-fitted suits, silently marched the office corridor. They were all department heads. Today had been in each of their diaries for months. It was the big test day where Dr Rivers would achieve the impossible. They had all been here three times prior. Three previous tests, each one ending in failure. Proceeding to the Subconscious Institutes' department of Combined Technologies, known to the public as Curative Analytical; they wondered it today's test would be any different.

The double doors opened onto a small balcony, which overlooked a large laboratory below. Dr Rivers was already there. A large computer screen was fixed to the balcony railings next to him.

"Dr Foster, Prof. Mielikki, Dr Samuels," Dr Rivers said as he turned his head to see his colleagues arrive.

"Doctor," Samuels and Foster replied in unison.

"So, today appears promising. If the last segments of data sets are to be believed," Dr Mielikki raised his brow.

"They're accurate and scalable. I can assure you. Over a hundred samples were collected to produce this data," Dr Rivers interjected.

"Oh, I'm aware of just how many samples, we've never produced this much Epsilac in one quarter, let alone these past few months," Mielikki continued.

"And we're still struggling to meet demand!" Dr Rivers remarked.

Their attentions were drawn upwards. Above the balcony, on the opposite wall, was a large frosted window. A light flicked on and a trio of dark silhouettes appeared at the window.

"The directors," Samuels gasped.

"You must be confident this time, Rivers," he added.

Dr Rivers smiled as he placed his long thin finger against the computer screen.

"Dr Frances, you may begin."

Dr Frances worked in the laboratory below. As he heard Dr Rivers's voice come through his earpiece, the middle-aged man flicked a few switches on a control panel next to him. Other scientists in the laboratory became more active and darted around, completing final checks and readying bits of equipment.

A huge screen, which sat on a free wall, came to life. The screen was larger than the balcony and the directors' window combined. As it came on, streams of ancient Greek numbers and letters raced in all directions across it.

"So, that's the new hard drive?" Dr Foster asked, as he pointed down at one of the scientists, who'd just pulled out an intricate glass structure, about the size of a pint glass.

"From here, it looks exactly the same as the last one," he continued.

"The intricacies of its structure, the microscopic indents and curvatures, are different. The main external design is for the interface, that is the same," Professor Mielikki explained.

"Exactly. Its inner design's not visible to the naked eye, even if you were down there," Rivers replied, not moving his eyes from the hard drive.

The four men watched as the scientist who carried the glass device, moved towards a modern looking computer interface. He placed the hard drive on a plinth that rested just below the computer screen. The scientist then connected two wires, which stretched from the computer onto two protruding nozzles that came out of the sides of the hard drive. As soon as it was connected, the numbers and letters racing across the screen stopped.

Dr Frances flicked a few more switches. The room darkened, and all the scientists in the lab moved to the edges and behind the safety screens. Dr Frances was still exposed, until he flicked one more set of switches. A four-sided protective screen rose from the ground and stopped just above his head.

"We're all set to begin the test, sir," Dr Frances said into his mouthpiece.

Dr Rivers heard the announcement come from his computer. He touched the reply button and uttered one simple command. "Begin."

Pressing buttons as soon as he heard the command, Dr Frances started up the interface. Instantly, the ceiling opened, and a large mechanical arm entered and gradually made its way down. Those on the balcony and the directors, watched.

The arm moved down slowly, stopping just above the hard drive. The top of the hard drive had a small nozzle that spiralled upwards. It was just one of the many external protuberances that gave this device its fascinating and unusual appearance.

A countdown rang out in a cold computer voice, "Five, four, three, two…one."

As the countdown ended, a small tube came out of the mechanical arm and gently made contact with the upwards nozzle of the hard drive. As soon as it connected, a dull, luminescent yellow liquid dribbled down the tube and into the hard drive.

The yellow liquid raced around the insides. The air around the device appeared distorted as a high-frequency hum rang out. Some in the room could hear it and quickly placed their hands over their ears.

The eerie atmosphere from the strange hum, the dull yellow glow, and the distorted air around the device, made the skin on the back of everyone's necks prickle. Suddenly, their attention shifted to the computer screen.

Once again, it raced with numbers and Greek letters. The sequence appeared random at first, then the pace of the streams got faster and faster until the image on the screen flicked, and a distorted map appeared. The map was topographical of the Earth, though it was hard to make out.

Different colour fogs seemed to spread out all over it. Dr Frances squinted. He quickly tapped on some keys, changing and amending some of the machine's settings. To his amazement, the fog receded. Soon, bright blue spots appeared at what looked like random locations on the map.

"Actual Seechers?" Samuels asked, leaning in towards Dr Rivers.

"Yes, Seechers, or those who could become Seechers," Rivers whispered.

"This is phenomenal, Rivers. It finally works!" Mielikki said as his face lit up.

Before Rivers could reply, the screen distorted. Now, green horizontal lines obscured the map.

"Ensure the system has recorded the location data. Change the frequency of the input to 2.2 megahertz," Dr Rivers shouted as he frantically tapped his screen.

Dr Frances jumped to follow his command. He lowered the input frequency, but the screen remained unchanged. He checked the system. It had already recorded everything on the screen a few moments before the interference.

The screen was now completely filled with flashing green lines. The hum, that was at first only audible to some, was now screeching and deafening all. The hard drive that once rested peacefully on the plinth, shook and jolted with the vibrations.

"Shut it off. Shut…it…off!" Doctor Rivers screamed.

Before anyone could act on the order, the hard drive exploded. Little shards of glass flew across the room, hitting safety screens on all sides. At some collision points, yellow light distorted the glass, which made it bulge and melt.

One large safety shield shattered, sending even larger chunks of razor-sharp plastic flying towards a group of scientists. Most of them fell to floor for cover. Shards struck a few them. An older scientist, who was too slow to escape, was hit directly in the neck. Blood spurted from his severed vein, and he slumped to the ground, splashing into a pool of his own blood.

Fortunately for the others in the room, the rest of the yellow liquid, which had, moments ago, been contained within the device, came into contact with nothing but air and quickly faded from existence.

"Damn it," Rivers said as his fist slammed hard on the balcony railings.

"Almost there, Rivers. I thought the Tauredunum texts said it was indestructible?" Samuel said smiling.

"Maybe next time," Foster gleefully muttered to Samuel.

The four men all noticed the directors' window light switch off and the silhouettes vanish. Foster and Samuels left the balcony to return to their own work, as Professor Mielikki joined Rivers. They looked down at the laboratory, as the scientists below rushed around in a hysterical state, trying to restrict the flow of blood, from the dying man's wound.

"It was close. It clearly worked for a moment there. We all saw that. You never know, there may be some useable data from it," Mielikki said.

"The location data will most likely be too vague to work out. You saw the maps. I'd be surprised if we can narrow it down to cities. It should have worked this time. I don't understand what went wrong," Rivers bit on his lip.

"Perhaps the combining of technologies like this is simply not possible. The Tauredunum technology, though impressive, is hundreds of years old. It was never designed to interface with 21st century equipment," Mielikki reasoned.

"I don't buy that. Of course, it's possible. The Tauredunum Raiders are the only group in history to have defeated the Seechers. And that's only down to their advanced development of anti-Seecher technology, designed solely to combat Seechers and their unnatural ways," Rivers glared at the floor, taking a moment to gather his thoughts. "I need more data."

"I'm not too sure more data collected from those who could become Seechers will help you."

"No, we need this. We need to be able to identify actual Seechers. How much longer do you think we'll stay off their radar for? Eventually, they'll track us down. The directors need a way of knowing the size and scale of what will inevitably confront us, if we don't strike them first," Rivers replied, a glint twinkling in his eye.

"Possibly. But the directors aren't going to want to fund this project of yours for too much longer. Your department gets nearly as much of the budget as the Omega Project," Mielikki scoffed.

Dr Rivers touched another button on his screen.

"Mark, I want you to ensure Dr Frances has saved all his work. Make sure his records are up to date. Then relieve him from his duties.

Appoint a new project lead. That Dr Pine is younger and more ambitious. Give him the job."

Mielikki dropped his jaw slightly as he heard Dr Rivers give out his orders on the intercom.

"I need to be going, the twelve o'clock extractions will begin soon," Mielikki said as he turned to walk off.

"The extraction process, I wonder if there are errors in that," Dr Rivers muttered under his breath.

Dr Rivers followed Mielikki off the balcony. The two men continued their conversation as they walked down a series of corridors. Entering new wings with swipes of their security cards, it wasn't long before they were in Mielikki's Medical Department.

"It could be that this is what's letting me down," Rivers said as they entered a room marked as the observation lounge.

"There's no more scope for improving our current procedure. I assure you, Rivers, the extraction process is as refined as it can be. The Epsilac we have provided for your experiment is the purest that can be produced."

A voice sounded from a speaker above them, "Extraction process of subject 987 will commence."

The two men looked out of the glass wall that covered one side of the observation lounge.

"Look for yourself, this is the most refined process for extraction ever devised."

The two men watched as an unconscious Stephen Monroe lay strapped to an examination table. His head was shaved and he wore a white hospital gown. Dripple trickled from his mouth. The straps were a dark brown leather. They fastened his wrists, ankles and six times across his body. Large machines sprung to life, rotating around him. He moved along the automated system, until coming to a stop. Then the table juddered, as it lifted him totally upright.

He slumped a little due to gravity, but the straps were so tight they kept him mostly still to the table. A deep hydraulic noise sounded, as another large machine-arm moved down from the ceiling and stopped just above his head. Red lights scanned his young lifeless face, before two large clamp-like fittings dropped down and locked his head into position, on either side.

Then a dark metallic drill rose from the floor, behind the upright table. The head of the drill had a long sharp, glistening needle at its centre. It moved up and stopped, just in line with the back of the subject's head. The top of the table retracted down, leaving Stephen's shaved head exposed to the needle.

Dr Rivers didn't flinch as the needle spun loudly, tearing through the skin and bone, drilling its way deep into the back of Stephen's head.

The drilling stopped, and a sucking vacuum sound was heard.

Behind the needle was a thin transparent tube, which carefully pulled a small amount of dull glowing yellow liquid from out of Stephen Monroe's head, and down through the tubing.

Frigid night air hit Aris's face. There was an eerie silence. His eyes gazed down over the building's edge and onto the water. *How high up am I?*

He couldn't recall how he'd made it to the top of this building nor why he was even there in the first place. He held something bright in his hands. His heart thumped. A familiar voice, rang out. Maya.

"STOP!"

He turned to face her. His face contorted, and his lips moved, but he couldn't hear a word he said. Just the empty sound of silence.

It wasn't long before men in black suits arrived at Maya's side. A charged conversation occurred. He was a part of it, but he had no idea what he was saying. It was like he was a visitor in his own body. And still, he could hear nothing. None of Maya's words, nor his own, were audible.

The scene continued to play out in a deathly muteness for a minute or more until a sudden and deafening shot rang out. Aris's heart leapt from his chest. It was the sound of a gun firing. A gun that was pointed at him. A gun held by Maya.

Aris stumbled forwards in slow motion. A searing pain formed in his back. It was the worst pain he'd ever experienced. The bullet ripped its course through his stomach. Just as the pain became all-consuming, unbearable, he woke.

Bolting upright in bed, Aris panted hard as sweat formed on his brow. "Just a dream, another crazy dream," he whispered to himself.

He felt clammy, and the bed was so hot, he threw off the sheets to try and cool down, remembering vividly how cold the rooftop in his dream had been. The room was draped in darkness, and Aris knew it was still the early hours of the morning. Far too early to think about getting up, but there was no chance of going back to sleep now either.

He lay uncovered in his bed, holding his stomach, staring at the ceiling, lost in the darkness. Trying to rationalize his dream.

Maya shot me! Why would she shoot me? Who were those men? Why did it feel so real?

Question after question came to him, but no answers appeared. Eventually, he calmed down. As his thoughts became still, he decided it was pointless to continue with the self-questioning. It was, after all, just a dream and, therefore, pointless to analyse.

Unless It wasn't…

Aris arrived at uni unusually early and found it a pleasant novelty to have spare time on his hands, instead of dashing straight to a lecture. He had spent most of his spare time caring for his dad. Though, today, he had made a special effort to try and catch Maya to make amends.

He walked into the union café, and after buying a gingerbread latte, Aris scanned the place for anyone else he may know, but no one was there. He found an empty table and sat. His mind raced with so many thoughts. Pep and his strange companions, the mirrored room, his dream. Concerns about where Stephen Monroe was.

He waited there for half an hour, until he finished his last mouthful of cold coffee and made his way out. On his way to the lecture theatre, he spotted Maya in the distance, making her way there, too.

Aris jogged towards her.

"Maya. Can I talk?"

"Clearly!" she replied, cold and thorny.

"Maya, please. Look I'm sorry. I can explain."

Maya turned her back on him. "I'm not in the mood."

Aris walked around to face her.

"Listen. I've so much to tell you," he pleaded.

"Tell me what?" Maya snapped.

"There's a lot," he mumbled.

"We have twenty minutes before the lecture," she said, looking at her watch.

"Maya, just forgive me. You've got it all—"

"Twenty minutes starts now, so talk fast. I'll work on forgiving you. Just talk."

The pair made their way into the building and found a small cubby area just outside the theatre. Aris explained to her how he went back to see Pep last night, and that he swore the doors locked by themselves. He went on to describe that Pep wasn't alone. That there were two others, and they talked about identifying people who they feared were being attacked or disappearing. And they were talking about Stephen Monroe. Aris finished by describing the peculiar mirrored-room and the mystery of Pep vanishing.

"Holy shit!" Maya exclaimed. "This is unbelievable! What you're saying is madness. So, he is a Seecher?!" She exhaled a few short hot breaths.

Aris nodded.

"He's definitely—" Maya stopped.

"Yes!"

"Fuck, I knew it!"

"What do we do now?" Aris looked into her eyes.

"We keep a tight watch on Pep. And you…you need to show me this mirrored room. Tonight!"

"We'd need a security card. Pep's security card. Like I said, there were doors he accessed with it. We won't be able to get into that room without one," Aris replied.

Maya thought hard. "You're right. We need to give that some thought. We could always try and follow him again. You were lucky not to get caught. Doing it again would need a lot more planning," Maya put a hand to her mouth.

"I thought you said there's no such thing as luck?" Aris smirked. giving her a prod.

"Don't be smart, Aris, it doesn't suit you. Come over to mine tonight. We'll decide a plan then. I've got an intern meeting this afternoon, so come over at eight. We'll get pizza. But, for now," Maya paused for a sharp calming breath, "keep your head down in this lecture. Don't act all genius, or psychic, or weird, or anything. But don't be stupid, either."

Aris raised an eyebrow. "How does one even do that?" Aris squeezed his lips tight.

"I don't know. Just don't talk! Unless you're asked a direct question, then obviously answer," Maya said as she looked at her watch. At that exact moment, the lecture theatre doors opened, and streams of young students filed out.

"So, did they agree with us?" Tallia Ward asked, as she poured clear tea into an elegant cup, which rested on a matching saucer. Tallia was the lady Pep was talking to, the night Aris overhead them in the lecture theatre. She was sympathetic-looking, with wavy strawberry-blonde hair and light eyes. She was in her forties and wore a pastel pink blouse and cardigan, which complemented her light complexion. She up-held a simple vegan diet; as being at peace with all living things was extremely important to her.

Pep watched as Tallia filled the cup. He waited until she'd placed the pot down before replying.

"Yes, of sorts. You know the Guild Elders rarely agree, not unanimously or in any steadfast fashion, anyway. They've agreed to not oppose our wish to break the cycle and complete our activation ceremonies early if…"

Tallia put her cup down. "If what?"

Pep drew a deep breath as he continued, "If there's a life-threatening need."

"So, not supporting the decision but not opposing it, either?" Tallia raised a brow.

"Exactly," Pep said as he poured milk into his cup. "You know how they don't like deviating from the rules, but they also don't like meddling with the internal affairs of individual guilds. If they can help it."

"Hmmm. But do they appreciate our need or not? What did they say about the unseen threat and the many disappearances?" Tallia asked.

"They acknowledge our reports of a threat are valid. They refute any notion it's the original enemy or the old enemy. They suggest it's a new threat. But since no guild can provide any solid information about them, nor produce any evidence as to the scale of the disappearances, the Elders are currently of the opinion the threat to us, and to Nihilo, stands as minimal," Pep took a long sip of his tea as he finished.

"Pompous old farts!" Tallia exclaimed.

Pep threw Tallia a disapproving look.

"Except for you, of course." Tallia held in a giggle.

"Of course."

Tallia sipped her tea, then leant in.

"So, when are we going to bring them in? We must act fast. Really, we should convene the whole London Guild first and brief them, then gather the Potentials for testing."

"I agree to convene active members. We can update silent parties later. As to whether we break the cycle?" Pep let out a deep sigh. "I'm still of two minds."

"Why?" she demanded.

"It's a massive undertaking."

"Their lives are in danger! It's in our hands to take responsible action, to protect them. We can't leave them out there for the wolves any longer, Pep!"

Pep finished his tea and observed the bottom of his cup, swirling it gently around, much like a tea-leaf reader would do.

"The risks of undergoing activation when they're not prepared is very high. Our history is littered with the crimes of those who've undergone activation too early and failed to adhere to the covenant. I will not be responsible for the creation of the next great threat," Pep looked into Tallia's eyes.

Tallia sat back with a grunt.

"Then we bring them in for testing and agree no activations will be conducted until we're absolutely convinced they're ready and in line with the covenant."

"Agreed," Pep replied.

"We're doing the right thing," Tallia reassured, as Pep looked out at the café window.

———

Maya sat at a circular table with four other interns. Only one of them she had met before, Robert Taylor. He was the UCL student who gave out flyers at university. He was an intern in the HR Department. The five of them all sat around the table in silence.

Maya kept glancing down at her watch. She was eager for time to pass and get home to see Aris. She wanted to plan how they could snare a Seecher. The door to the room unexpectedly burst open as a tall, stern-looking man entered.

"Good afternoon, all. My name is Dr Rivers. I'm Head of Combined Technologies here at Curative Analytical. And I am here to offer one of you a fantastic future opportunity."

The five interns glanced at each other with wide eyes before returning their attention to the doctor. Maya scanned the man as she squirmed in her seat.

"You're here today because you five are our top interns within the whole organization. Some of you have demonstrated real promise. Now, I have one vacancy in my department, and I'm looking for the best of the best. I'm going to give you the opportunity to take that post, whenever you want it," Dr Rivers towered over them.

There was a small gasp amongst the group.

"Am I being moved from Medical Applications?" asked one of the interns.

"Yes. You'll all be moving under my department for the time being. It's one of the more confidential and exciting areas of our work. You'll all get a chance to prove yourselves over here," Rivers turned his attention to the open door.

"Simon, in you come," he bellowed.

A broad and menacing man entered the room. He wasn't as tall as Dr Rivers, but his appearance was physically more intimidating. He carried five files and five passes attached to lanyards. He handed them out.

"These are you passes. In your files, you'll find a confidentiality agreement, which you need to read and sign before you leave. If you don't agree to the terms, then this opportunity's not for you," Dr Rivers said as Simon left the room.

The group quickly glanced through the paperwork and signed. Not one of them had truly read each line of the long contract. Maya paused just after signing the document and flicked back to an earlier page.

"Excuse me. It says here we're going to work on some sensitive data that's not to be shared and can only be worked on within the premises. It states the data requires deciphering. Will this be similar to the profile data I worked on in the Analytical Department?" Maya asked.

"It's data that will need defining and deciphering. It will be challenging. All we know is that the data relates to geographical locations that need unscrambling," Dr Rivers replied, smiling.

"Okay, you'll all be expected to work a full day tomorrow, nine to five. After that, you'll be free to work on it as you see fit. But remember, the one who demonstrates the fastest progress and clearest solutions will be the one in line for the job. Now, excuse me. I must attend a meeting. Simon will show you out," Dr Rivers finished.

Aris looked at the time and closed his laptop. He tossed it on his bed, grabbed his jacket, and darted down the stairs. His dad was back home and sat at the kitchen table, eating his dinner.

"Dad, I'm off. Do you need anything?" Aris placed a hand gently on his shoulder.

"My meds and my book," his dad replied.

Making his way into the lounge Aris scanned the coffee table for his dads' medications and his book. The medications were set out in a weekly Dossett pack, and Aris quickly disconnected the evening's drugs from the rest of the pack. He moved the newspapers and letters around, searching for the book his dad wanted.

"You know the hospital said to call them if you get a fever or have any difficulty breathing."

In the other room, Peter rolled his eyes. "I know, I know."

Lifting some letters from the table, Aris noticed bold red writing on one of them. He placed everything else down and unfolded the bill.

"You know, you're lucky they let you out today," Aris shouted.

"They needed the bed. Bloody cheapskates our government. Kicking a dying man out of a hospital bed."

Reading the council tax bill, Aris's jaw dropped when he saw that it was a final warning and his dad owed the council nearly seven hundred pounds. Aris quickly looked through the other letters, and it was clear his dad owed just under two thousand pounds, with companies issuing him with final notices.

Taking the bills, the book, and the medications, Aris walked into the dining area and placed all of them in front of his dad.

"Why didn't you tell me that your finances were this bad?"

Clutching the bills and bringing them close, Peter ground his jaw. "This is private. You shouldn't be reading my post. God damn you, Aris. I have no privacy anymore, since you've moved back in."

"I'm here for you. Not for me. This affects us both," Aris snapped.

"No. It's my problem, I'll sort it out," Peter replied, putting the letters under his arm.

"How? Where are you going to get that kind of money from?"

"I'll think of something. I always have. You don't need to worry," Peter returned to eating his dinner as if nothing had happened.

"Gambling's not the answer," Aris muttered. Peter slammed his palm down on the table.

"How dare you speak to me like that," Peter spat.

"I can drop out of university and get a job to pay for us both, Dad. Maybe that's what needs to happen."

"Your mother would never allow it. She wanted you to go to university."

"She's not here anymore. You've got to stop hanging onto the past like this and how mum wanted it to be. Stop sitting around this house spending all your time thinking back to how great things were. I can sort these bills out. But you have to stop betting what you have on horses. You need to think about the future. You're not a dying old man, you've had a scare, that's all." Aris let out a deep breath as he made his way to the front door.

"Come back! Don't you dare speak to me like that," Peter shouted after Aris.

Aris ignored his dad as he grabbed his jacket and deliberately slammed the front door shut. He had a solution in his mind of how he was going to sort out the finances. He took out the crumbled Curative Analytical flyer from the inner pocket of his jacket.

Easy money, he thought.

———

"What's with the face, Aris? You look like someone's killed your dog." Aris didn't respond. "Shit, you don't have a dog, do you?!" Maya opened the door to Aris.

"No dog," Aris said as he slumped in and looked up. "Wow, nice house."

"Thanks. Come in." Maya closed the door. The house was grand, with a large collection of old clocks.

"Cool, what's with all the clocks?"

"Oh, my dad collects them, has done for years." Maya guided Aris into the dining room.

The dining room was plush, with a large wooden dining table and six impressive hand-carved chairs. An ostentatious chandelier hung from the ceiling.

Maya pulled out a chair.

"Is it just you and your dad here?" Aris asked as he sat down.

"Yeah. Well, it's usually just me. My dad works a lot. I can go days without seeing him. I'm not even sure if he's back home tonight or not." Maya shrugged.

"Oh."

"Why are you down? What's up?" Maya sat opposite him.

"Dad's back from hospital today, and the first thing we do is have an argument."

"About what?"

"Money." Aris threw a fake smile her way. Maya nodded before standing up again.

"How about a drink and some pizza? You up for that? Might make you feel better," Maya made her way to the open kitchen.

He sat there, eyes glazed.

"Hey, Aris. Drink? Pizza?"

"Oh…yeah. Coke would be great. I'm starving. I'll eat anything that doesn't have mushrooms on it," he replied. Maya left the room and returned with two Cokes, along with some blank paper and pens. She placed them on the table and sat next to Aris.

"Right, let's start off by going over everything you heard again. I'll make notes so we've got a record. Then we'll formulate a plan on how we're going to break into the mirrored room," Maya wrote down the heading: *Aris's Encounter*.

Aris described what he'd heard again. The two strange voices, the fact they talked about missing people. How they had mentioned Stephen Monroe, and even Aris's name had been discussed. Maya punched him in the arm and demanded to know why he hadn't told her that before. Continuing in as much detail as possible, Aris described the corridors, the doors and, finally, the mirrored room.

Maya scribbled this all down as fast as Aris spoke, capturing everything he said. When he finished, he considered telling her about the dream he'd had about her, the one where she shoots him, but decided against it, from fear of sounding too peculiar.

"We need to find out more about Stephen, like…where he is exactly. Why would Leo say he's at his brothers, yet the Seechers think he's been kidnapped?!"

They stared deeply into each other's eyes.

"I don't know what to believe. I also find it weird that both me and Thomas have dreamt about people being kidnapped. I can't help but think the dreams might be more than just dreams now," Aris looked down at his hands.

"Okay, my head's whirling. We need food. I'm gonna order the pizza now," Maya pulled out her phone and brought up a number.

"Oh, what? I thought you ordered it already."

"I'm doing it now," Maya walked into the kitchen to speak to the man on the other end.

As she did, Aris looked over her notes. She'd written so much detail. He looked back up at her and watched her while she spoke on the phone. She hadn't immediately noticed, but as soon as she'd finished, she turned and glared back at him.

"Stop with the vacant looks."

"Sorry," Aris muttered as he quickly looked back down at the notes.

"What about our plan to get you into the mirrored room? Our best opportunity has to be after PP Club. Right? At least then, it'll be late, and the university's quieter."

Aris picked up a pen and jotted this down.

"Agreed, it's an excellent time for it. Can you phone Leo and get to the bottom of where Stephen is? I can't wrap my head around the fact that he might have been kidnapped! That just seems ridiculous."

Maya returned to her seat and took the pen and sheets of paper from Aris.

"I texted Leo on my way here. Still nothing. I'll call him after we eat and find out what's going on. He's been really quiet, too." Aris took his phone out of his pocket and put it on the table.

"Good. We also need to work out how we get a security card. We could always try the classic distract and steal technique," she finished.

"Have *you* tried calling Stephen's phone? I don't have his number." Aris tapped his phone.

Before either of them could continue, the front door unlocked. Maya's face dropped. She quickly whispered, "Hide those. That's my dad."

Aris folded the pile of paper in half and put it in his pocket.

Maya got to her feet and made her way to the hallway to greet her father. His voice called out, "Maya, are you in? I'm home!"

Aris jumped up out of his chair. His heart pounded so hard he put his hand to his chest and took a few deep breaths.

"Maya?" The voice filled the house again. He knew that voice.

"Hey, Dad. Yeah, I'm here. My friend Aris is over. We're just doing some uni work together. I didn't know you were coming home today!" Aris shuffled around on his own. He sat back down. Stood up. Sat back down.

"Oh, very good. Well, don't mind me. Let me come and say hello. It's always nice to meet your friends." The voice was no longer at a distance. It was close, entering the room.

Aris turned on his chair to watch. Sweat began to fall from his brow. His hands clammed up. Saliva raced to his mouth. He gulped it down as a tall and smartly-dressed middle-aged man walked in alongside Maya.

"You should have called, dad. I would have ordered you a pizza," Maya smiled towards Aris, then quickly frowned.

"Oh, don't worry about me. I'll make my own dinner," Maya's dad placed his jacket down. "Good Evening. Aris, is it? I'm Adam." He nodded as he offered his hand.

Aris wiped his palm on his trousers before he shook it, uttering a single word, "Sir."

"Are you okay?" Adam asked.

"I'm not feeling well." Aris awkwardly rose to his feet and moved towards Maya.

"I'm sorry, I have to go. I feel a bit peculiar. It's my stomach. It happens sometimes. We can do this tomorrow, Maya," Aris held his tummy with his hands and quickly made his way to the front door. Maya followed.

"Aris, what's up?" She asked.

"It's nothing. Honestly. Speak tomorrow. Good night." Aris took the paper out of his pocket and stuffed it into her hands.

Maya stared as Aris jogged down the path before turning onto the road and running off.

"He seems very odd," Adam remarked as he joined Maya's side.

"Very odd indeed," Maya agreed, hidding the notes behind her back.

———

Aris finally stopped running a few streets away. He leant down, with his hands on his thighs, and panted heavily.

"It can't be. It just can't," he whispered to himself.

His mind filled with questions, and with each intake of breath and more clarity of thought, he couldn't dispel the truth that was right in front of him. How and when was he going to tell Maya. *She must know? How can she not know? She'd guessed it of her mother.* The answers where not forthcoming. He found himself speaking aloud as the frightening realization presented itself clearly.

"Maya's dad is the man Professor Maxwell was talking to. Maya's dad's a Seecher!"

THROUGH THE
LOOKING MIRROR

Maya walked into the elevator with the other four interns. She glanced down at her phone. She'd sent Aris several text messages since his abrupt departure from her house last night, but he'd still not replied. No text, no call, nothing.

"You'll need to hand that to the desk on the eighth floor when we get there. No personal phones are permitted in the Combined Technologies Department," Simon instructed, on seeing Maya engrossed in her screen. She promptly turned the screen blank and gave Simon a sheepish look. The elevator went up.

Apart from the ground floor and the Library that was located on the basement level, Maya had never seen anything else of the building where she'd interned for nearly ten weeks now. The lift doors opened onto the eighth level and Simon was first to leave.

"Remember, you'll need to use your pass for the lift, and it will only give you entry to this level." He ushered them out and directed them to a desk situated directly opposite the elevator. They went over and signed a ledger, placed the lanyards over their heads, and handed in their mobile phones. Maya gave hers one last look before she handed it in.

"So, we're going through the doors to the right. This wing, including the three floors above, are all part of the Combined Technologies. And that there," Simon stopped for a brief second as he turned and pointed towards the double doors on the left-hand side, "that leads to another essential part of the business. That's Medical Applications. Your card doesn't give you access to that side because you're not permitted to enter it. So, don't try!" As he finished, he walked towards the doors to the right. He swiped his card and directed the rest of them to follow him. They entered the Combined Technologies Department.

They walked past individual offices and small laboratories, which were scattered along the corridor. As they neared the end of the hall, Maya saw a large double door which appeared locked. This too had a security pass strip, to gain entry.

"This is our main laboratory. You can't access it, but perhaps if you're lucky enough then, one day, you'll end up working in there. That's frontier science, right there. What happens in there's going to change the world," Simon said, turning in front of the doors.

The five young faces shone.

"Right, so you're all going to be based in this office over here," Simon said as he opened a door to his left, directing the interns in. They entered with broad smiles on their faces. The room was filled with scientists so absorbed in their own work that they didn't even have time to acknowledge the newcomers.

"Morning." A smartly-dressed lady with a cheerful smile made her way towards them.

"People, this is Jane Goodswell. She'll be your supervisor. If you have any problems, direct them to her." Simon didn't wait for the interns to reply, nor for Jane to accept the handover. He simply turned around and headed out, saying, "Good luck," with a perfunctory wave of his hand.

"Hello, hello! Lovely to meet you all. Let me show you to your desks. Then I'll give you each a copy of the data. I've managed to produce some decipher keys I hope you'll find helpful. Although they're basic and only produce limited results, at least it'll get you started. You'll have to work out the rest on your own." Jane ended her speech with a nervous giggle.

She directed the interns to individual booths and distributed the data packs. Maya was quick to bring up the information on her computer. It wasn't anything like the numerical data she'd worked on before. The one on her screen was strange. A few ancient Greek letters and symbols were embedded in it.

"That's really odd," Maya remarked to herself.

Maya ran the deciphering keys Jane had provided. She wasn't surprised that it produced very little additional insight. Looking though both the original data and some of the output from the decoded materials, Maya slowly leaned back in her chair.

The sun beat down through Aris's bedroom window. It was nearly one o'clock in the afternoon when Aris finally got out of bed. He hadn't slept well. It wasn't until three in the morning before he eventually drifted off to sleep. His night was filled with fractured sleep and littered with recurring dreams.

He had been in Oxford, on top of the roof of that big office building, and even dreamt of being in a London Underground tube station. *No wonder I've slept in so late. This dreaming's a full-time job,* he thought. He had had a long and strange conversation about Stephen with Leo the night before. Leo was adamant Stevo had a lot of personal issues due to his mental health, and that he was away dealing with them. Aris didn't want to push Leo any further on the topic. Leo was stressed with his exams and thought the last few had gone badly, and he was having to re-learn his year-two books again.

Making his way downstairs and into the kitchen, Aris made himself a cup of tea as he watched the sunshine outside of the window. He knew his dad was in the front room, but he couldn't bring himself to engage in conversation right now. The phone rang in his pocket.

"Hello. Yes, speaking. Oh, yes. I did, last night," Aris said with a yawn into his phone.

"Tomorrow? Wow. That's quick. I could be. What times do you have available?" he paused as he listened to the lady on the other end offering appointment times.

"Two thirty. Yes, perfect, I can do that. It's near Embankment, is that right? Great. Three hours and a blood sample. That's fine. Yes, I'll be there. Thank you. Goodbye," Aris finished the call and picked up his tea. He headed straight back to his room.

Perched on the edge of his bed, he flipped open his laptop. Switching it on, he opened a new word document. The cursor flashed. He knew why he'd opened the document, but to make a start, to write anything, was difficult. Taking a large gulp of tea, he typed with one hand. He wished he could tell someone else about it. Talk it out with a friend. But it was too sensitive a topic to tell anyone about and far too unbelievable. *Perhaps Thomas would understand*, he thought. But his strong sense of loyalty towards Maya, to keep her knowledge of the Seechers a secret, meant he would never say anything behind her back.

Dear Maya. He typed. Then deleted it again. *I'm sorry…*he typed again. Then deleted.

Letting out a sigh, he picked up his phone, tapped in his password, and brought up the messages from her. She'd text him eight times. He read through them again, looking for an angle from where to start.

"Some genius," he said as he threw his phone onto his bed. "I don't even know what to say." He thought for a moment as he bounced his leg. Then tried typing that. But as soon as he had written it, he deleted it again and just started at the blank screen. He sat up, took a deep breath, and just typed his stream of consciousness…

The problem is I'm not sure if being a Seecher is a good thing or a bad thing. And every time this happens, I'm drunk. What if I'm just making it up? But I wasn't drunk when I saw Pep's reflection that time at the hospital. Could he have been there, without being there? Why did he say he was looking out for me? I'm not in any danger or anything….am I?

———

"Morning, Tulip. You're up early. Did you have trouble sleeping?" Adam asked as he made himself a coffee from an elaborate cafetière.

Maya sat at the table, swirling her spoon around a bowl of cereal.

"Maya, are you okay?" Adam said as he moved to the table, his fresh coffee steaming.

Raising her head to watch her dad take a seat, Maya curled her lips down.

"Yes, I'm fine. Just thinking," she lied.

"Thinking about what? The internship? Oh, my gosh, the job opportunity?! I'm so proud of you. You know that, don't you? You've achieved so much already," Adam said as he placed his hand on hers.

Maya's face didn't reveal much.

"Yes, that and uni and other things," Maya said, pulling her hand free from her dad's.

"By other things…do you mean, boys?" Adam asked, fully prepared for her response.

"Oh, God. No. Just no. Don't," Maya said as she stood up and took her bowl. "We haven't got that kind of relationship, Dad, where we talk of such things." As she finished, she walked to the kitchen, emptied her bowl and placed it into the dishwasher. Adam smiled at her reply.

"Thanks for trying, though," Maya said as she walked back into the dining room.

"You know, if you ever did want that kind of relationship, I'm happy to give it a try."

Maya paused for a moment.

"Thanks. I'll bear that in mind," she replied. "Right, I should really get going, I have a lecture at ten."

"Right. I'm going to head into the office soon, as well. Are you off to that talk in Oxford this weekend? With your university club, didn't you say?" Maya nodded. Adam continued. "I know I'm away a lot, Maya, but I just found out that next weekend I'll be away again for two weeks. For work. Things have got a little busy, and it looks like we've got a big job coming up. So, it's all hands-on deck."

Maya smiled.

"So, whilst I'm away, I'll get in plenty of food, leave you some cash, and arrange for the cleaner to come in twice as much," Adam said as he rose to his feet.

"Ha. Very kind of you. Thank you, but you don't have to feel bad about it. You know I'll be fine."

―――――

Aris sent the message. He couldn't hang on any longer. Although the text was designed as a holding message, it at least broke the silence.

– Look, I'm SORRY, Maya. I've been sorting things out in my head. This whole Seechers stuff has come as a big shock, and I'm not sure what to believe

about it. I'm also pretty caught up with my dad, as well. I'm sorry not to reply sooner. Thanks for understanding.

Maya read the words as they came through and quickly replied.

- Rude!

He glared at the one-word response for a few moments before noticing the icon at the bottom of the screen, indicated that Maya was still typing. Then her full reply came through.

— Well, you could've just said that without being all weird. I've not heard from you for nearly two days! Stephen hasn't replied to any of my calls or texts. I'm actually really worried. What are we meant to do? Where are you? Why aren't you in this lecture?

Aris took some time to collect his thoughts. He was meant to be in the lecture but had already sent his apologies to the lecturer for his absence. He was taking his dad to a doctor's appointment, and then he had to go to his own appointment at two thirty.

— Not in at all today. Going to the doctor's with dad this morning. Have a meeting later. I'm going tomorrow, though. You're still going right?

Maya's reply was instant.

— Is he okay? Yes, of course, I'm going!

— He'll be fine, thanks. Routine check-ups and tests. I'll see you tomorrow.

He didn't plan to tell her exactly where he was going. It was too humiliating to admit. Aris pressed send, then placed his phone down. He needed to get his dad ready and support him to the hospital. He threw a few things in his bag. Packing everything for the day, as he knew that after he dropped his dad back, he would have to leave straight away for his afternoon appointment at Curative Analytical.

———

"You're going to sit next to me, and we're going to sit away from the rest of the group," Maya said as she passed Aris, who watched the train as it came into the station. He thought for a moment about challenging her, but he knew his protests would be ignored and, at the least, he owed her some sort of explanation.

"I thought we had assigned seats?" Aris muttered.

"I'll find us more appropriate ones," Maya stated, not looking at

Aris. She simply waited for the train to come to a halt before she opened the door and stepped in.

Aris followed closely behind Maya as she made her way down the carriage. Each seat was marked as reserved. Entering the next carriage, they were both surprised and relieved to see it was nearly empty. Maya spotted two seats in the corner that would be ideal for their secretive discussions.

"There," Maya said as she pointed.

She continued to lead as Aris tailed behind. They sat down, and Maya yanked her notebooks out.

"You're a complete troglodyte, you know," Maya said, not looking at him.

"Wow…" Aris said open-mouthed. "I guess I deserved that. Look, I've said I am sorry. What more can I do?"

"Aris, you turned completely peculiar at my house. And now I've finally got you, you're going to tell me why," Maya eventually turned to face him.

Aris looked into her perfect blue eyes, which were burrowing into his soul.

"I'm sorry. I've a lot going on, and it's all become a bit too much. Things with my dad…" he stopped mid-speech to whisper, "the Seechers," then continued at normal volume. "And you can be rather intense at times." As he lied, he could hear his inner voice saying, *believe me, Maya, please, believe me.*

"Alright. Don't go on and on," Maya snapped. "If you do have another crisis moment, just tell me. Everyone has them, Aris. No need to be a wimp about it."

Aris smiled at Maya's harsh words. "Fine."

"Good. Well, I've been thinking more of how we gain access to the mirrored room. We know we need an activated card, but it doesn't have to be his, does it?"

"Well, no, it just needs to be one that has access to that hallway and the doors. But if not the professor's, then whose?" Aris asked.

"I haven't got that far yet. But he can't be the only one with a card that can access that room. It's a university, surely other lecturers can access that hallway. It's just a card with an electronic passcode on it," Maya opened up a page in her journal. The title read: *Getting to the Mirrored Room.*

"I guess. But who? I can't think of any other lecturer," Aris replied.

"What about the two voices? Do you think they were also lecturers?" Maya asked as Aris's leg jiggled. He pressed his leg down with his hand.

"I'm sure the woman said she worked or lived in Oxford," Aris recalled.

"Well, that's where we're going now! Keep your ears out for her. Maybe you'll recognize her voice again." Maya flicked back to the notes she'd written from Aris's account. "What about the guy? Anything about him that indicates he works at our uni, too?"

Aris gulped. "Maya, I don't think he works our at university. I'm almost certain he doesn't. You see, there's something I need to tell you. The guy, the one I overhead twice before…the first time…" Aris was unable to finish his sentence because the automatic doors opened, and Thomas and Abi burst into their carriage.

"There you are!" Abi shouted.

"Why aren't you down there with the group? Pep keeps asking after you, Aris. He wants to make sure you're on the train," Thomas said as the two neared.

Aris froze, his hands clammed up, and the blood in his face started to drain.

"Sorry, guys, we just needed to clear up a disagreement we had. Didn't want to do it in front of the whole group, you know what I mean," Maya said as she closed her books and slid them back into her bag. Thomas and Abi sat in the two seats in front, then turned and leant over the tops to talk to them.

"You guys fell out?" Abi asked.

"It's resolved now," Maya said, subtly elbowing Aris.

"Ha! I think we've all grown fond of having you around, Aris. It would be a shame to have to scrape your remains off the ground if you were ever to try and disagree with Maya," Abi said as she smiled at Maya.

"Oh, gosh, this isn't another broken heart. Maya, you're serial," Thomas joked. "Hey, Aris. Are you even there, man?" Thomas waved his hand directly in front of Aris's face.

"Yeah, sorry. Ermm, we're still not entirely clear what's really happened to Stephen. Leo's buried in his books, and we're not getting any concrete answers about his whereabouts. Do you know anything else?" Aris replied as he shook himself alert.

"Yeah. Leo finally showed me the text Stevo sent him. He's got bipolar and had to check himself into a clinic. It's a bit sad really. He asked Leo to lie to us about it. Must be why it wasn't sitting right. He'll be okay." Aris and Maya looked at each other and frowned.

"Hey, Thomas, tell Aris about the dream you had last night," Abi chirped. The train came to a stop at a platform, and a conductor gave out a message on the intercom about changing for this station.

"Go on." Aris sat up.

"Fine," Thomas succumbed. "It was short, but intense, like it was real life. I was in a room with a window, and there was this *tap, tap*. I got up, opened the window, and in flew a beautiful blue and green scarab beetle. It few around me. It felt like some sort of sign, you know? About destiny."

"Is that it?" Maya waved her hands.

"No, there's more. Well, not about Thomas's dreams but about the beetle," Abi interjected.

"What do you mean?" Airs asked.

"Well, how Thomas described the beetle, tapping on the window and flying around him, is almost exactly what happened to me last night. I kid you not. It wasn't a dream. An actual scarab beetle tapped on my window. I let it in, and it flew into my room. True story."

"No way," Maya exclaimed.

"No, I believe her. As I was describing my dream to her earlier, I could tell by her face, how she reacted, that something had happened, and when she told me, it just fit in with all the other weird stuff happening lately," Thomas whispered.

"That seriously happened to you last night?" Aris asked Abi.

"Yes. Exactly like that. The beetle came into my room. It sparkled and glowed this beautiful blue colour. I tried to catch it, but it got away. Damn, I should have caught it." Abi hit her fist on the top of the seat.

"Guys, something is seriously messed up. Too many strange things are happening," Aris murmured.

"You don't think our dreams are more than just dreams, do you, Aris? You think those dreams about those people being kidnapped actually happened?" Thomas asked.

Before Aris replied, he turned to look at Maya.

"I don't know, Thomas. If you asked me a couple of months ago, I would have laughed your crazy notion off. But lately, I can't help but think…maybe there is more to our dreams than we know," Aris whispered as the other three listened intently.

The train pulled away rather sharply, and both Abi and Thomas fell back a little. They both swiftly turned and fell into their seats. Aris leant into Maya. "You okay?"

"Yes. I'm fine. That's weird, right?"

"Yeah."

"All these things can't just be a coincidence," she insisted. She lowered her voice to continue. "What were you going to tell me, about that other man Pep was talking to?"

Aris's eyes widened. "Oh, crap," he gestured to the two in front. "I'll tell you another time."

———

The weekend had been thrilling for Maya, she had met an extremely inspiring and intellectual professor, had formulated plans with Aris about how to get in the Mirror Room and even managed to come up with some ideas on how to decipher the data that she was assigned to decode at the Department of Combined Technologies. Their talks of dreams had died down, as they became fascinated instead with Nagal's thoughts.

It had been over five days since she had met Thomas Nagal and listened to his fascinating talk entitled – 'Accounting for the Evolution of Consciousness.' It was interesting to hear concepts about the function and purpose of consciousness and the possible reasons for its development.

Maya had gone over the notes she had from Nagal's session many times these last few days, but today was Thursday, which was the day she was free of lectures. She had decided to go in and spend time on her internship work.

Jane had remarked that she hadn't seen Maya for nearly a week when she arrived. Maya ignored her and went straight to her new desk. She took out a recently purchased notebook and opened it to the only page that had anything written on it. A series of short sequence numbers, with written explanations in brackets.

Maya got to work fast. She used her notes as a guide and opened-up various deciphering programs on the company's intranet system. She completed her first key within a couple of hours, and she had started running it through the data whilst she worked on her next one.

The first program she had running ended and from the resulting data it was clear it was unsuccessful. It produced nothing noteworthy or workable. Maya wasn't too concerned as she looked over the findings, because she still had two more programs running and was already half-way through working on her fourth.

Time ticked on. She skipped lunch as she was determined to get all four of her ideas going. The results of her second seemed a little more promising but, ultimately, it was still indistinguishable nonsense. It was nearing five thirty, and the place was getting quieter and quieter as each hour passed. The fourth program was ready to launch, but Maya knew it would take over two hours for it to process, and she didn't want to stay too late tonight. Her dad was off tomorrow, for a couple of weeks, and they had dinner plans. She needed to be home by eight.

"Should I wait? I could come back tomorrow night. I have all week-end," she said to herself. As she finished, she looked at the running clock of her third program. It was ninety-eight percent complete and would finish in minutes.

She made her way to a vending machine, bought an energy drink, and returned to her desk just as the third program loaded its findings.

"Shit!" Maya gasped as she flung herself into the seat. "That looks promising." She moved the cursor and scrolled through some of the data. It was still largely a document filled with numbers, but at the end of each packet of information were definable words and structures.

Maya went through the information and compiled it in order of relevance and placed it into a folder.

In a separate document, Maya copied the deciphered information. She wasn't too sure what it meant or if was fully complete. Each entry followed the exact same sequence of a place name followed by numbers and letters, but they were still garbled and appeared meaningless.

London, 18T43P
Cambridge 2T5P
Bristol 1T2P
Manchester 3T6P
Birmingham 1T11P
Cardiff 3P
Edinburgh 1T4P
Glasgow 4T8P

Maya stood up and sent her findings off to the printer as she shouted over to Jane, who had just started packing her stuff up for the day.

"What is it?" Jane asked as she made her way over.

"I've got something," Maya replied.

Jane went through Maya's original output data and the compiled work. Her eyes grew wide as she reviewed the output.

"This looks good. Really good. We should show it to Dr Rivers right now. Stay here."

As soon as Jane finished talking, she was gone. Moments later, she returned with the doctor.

"This intern here, Maya, she's produced something rather interesting," Jane said as she walked over to the desk.

Dr Rivers sat in Maya's chair, not acknowledging her at all. He scanned through the information and as he got further through it, a cold smiled creeped onto his pale etched face.

"Excellent work," he said, looking over at Maya. "This is promising. Do you see anything more detailed in the output, like specific locations rather than just cities?" Dr Rivers asked, knowing the answer before he had asked it.

"I don't think so. They all have more data following the entries, but it's the same sequence. Therefore, it doesn't relate to anything more detailed. Not more information on specific locations," Maya replied.

"Smart girl. I agree. Shame. It's probably still worth the effort, though. Jane, share her key with everyone else. Get them all working on refining it." The doctor stood up.

"That's my key. It's not…"

Dr Rivers turned to her, and she paused.

"Don't fret, young lady. Come with me," Dr Rivers asked as he pushed the door open.

Maya quickly followed as they went into the opposite room.

"This is the main office where the seniors work. They have access to the company's mainframe. Unfettered access," Dr Rivers said as he arrived at Simon's desk. Maya stopped as she watched him tower over Simon. "Your key card," Dr Rivers held out his hand as he spoke. Maya gingerly gave it to him and watched him hand it over to Simon.

"Give this one access to this room and give her desk K7. She deserves it," Dr Rivers told Simon before turning to look at Maya. "You can count that job as yours. Congratulations. You did good work with that data. It was no mean feat. From now on, I want you to work in this office, near me. You demonstrate excellence and promise, and I want you to be fully aware that success is rewarded here."

Maya listened to Dr Rivers, but she struggled to look at him. Her eyes were fixed on Simon and the key card machine he used. She watched as he entered the card into the device and updated the access on his computer.

"Thank you, sir. I'm eager to decipher more of that information," she said.

"Forget that data. I'm going to get you working on another project for me. Working with some of the greatest minds in Europe. You're going to be working directly under Dr Pine. He's developing frontier science. You might even get to enter the main laboratory."

Dr Rivers took the time to show Maya to her new, much larger desk, in a side cubicle. Maya glanced at her watch. It was quarter to seven. She needed to make her way home. She thanked Dr Rivers and departed. She left via the reception on level eight, collected her phone and switched it on when she was in the elevator. It beeped with an unexpected text. It was from Aris.

Call me, please. My dad's in hospital again. I could really do with a friend right now.

It was approaching half-seven when Maya made it to the hospital. Aris had talked to her briefly on the phone and waited for her outside the ward. As the elevator at the end of the corridor opened, Aris turned and watched as Maya came out. He smiled for the first time that day.

"I'm so sorry. I was at work all day, and they don't allow any phones whilst we're there. How's he doing?" Maya bellowed as she hurried down the empty hallway.

"Thank you, Maya. It frightened the shit out of me this morning, getting a call from the doctor, telling me to call an ambulance right away and get him in," Aris replied as soon as she was close enough to hear him without the need for him to shout.

"Why did the doctor call? He's okay now, right?" Maya asked as she moved in to give Aris an unexpected hug.

Aris relished the intimate moment for as long as possible.

"It's something they found in his blood tests from last week. Apparently, his sodium is low and his white blood cells are high. They just told me he needed to come in for some treatment and more tests. So, here we are, again." Aris sighed.

"Best place for him, though. He's getting the help he needs, right?"

"Yes, I guess. At least they'll make sure he takes his medication on time, and it's not like he can gamble in here!" Aris sat down on one of the chairs in the corridor.

Maya sat down next to him and placed a light comforting hand on to his leg. "Aris, your dad will be fine. I'm sure you have plenty of years ahead of worrying about him. Our dads were put on this earth to create us, and then torment us, I'm sure of it."

Aris looked up and down the hallway. It was quiet, and no one else was around.

"Are you okay?" Maya put her hand on his.

"You keep asking me that," Aris rolled his eyes. "And since that night—"

"What night?" Maya frowned.

"I need to tell you something. I've not been entirely honest with you."

"Tell me what?"

"I'm sorry. I am. I've been struggling with this for ages, and even now, when there's absolutely no chance of *not* telling you, I'm finding it almost impossible to do so. I nearly told you on Saturday on the train, but I didn't. I wanted to. I just couldn't. And it's been eating me up ever since."

"Tell me what? Aris, just tell me!" Maya demanded. "It's fine, just tell me."

Maya watched as Aris's expression became tense. Maya closed her eyes, moved towards him, and placed her soft enviable lips against his.

The kiss was a shock, but it also left his entire body tingling with pleasure. As Maya moved back, he glanced deeply into her eyes as they both smiled contently, then Aris leant in, and they kissed again. Aris stopped for a second, dropped his head, then looked back up to Maya again.

"Your dad's the other Seecher."

"What?" she said as she scrunched-up her entire face.

"Your dad is the other man. The one I heard that night in the lecture hall with Pep and the woman. I'm sorry to have to tell you this. And I'm sorry I didn't tell you sooner."

Maya jumped to her feet.

"You're wrong. He would have told me. He would have. I know he would've. He couldn't keep something like that about himself from me," she said as Aris stood up beside her.

"I'm sorry. I don't know why he hasn't told you, but I am one hundred percent certain he's the other man. It was your dad's voice I heard, on both those nights."

"You're wrong, Aris. He's not a Seecher, my mum was! My dad can't be. He just can't be."

"Why could they not both be? Doesn't that make a lot of sense?"

"I've got to go," Maya said as she raced off. Aris sunk into the chair.

"What have I done?" he asked himself.

For the next few minutes, Aris stayed sat on the chair, wondering if he'd made a horrible mistake sharing that information with her. He took out his phone and called her. But she didn't answer.

"I better go after her," he whispered.

He got up to make his way down the stairs, but before he took a single step, a distinct female voice spoke from nowhere.

"No, Aris. No."

Turning around to see where the voice had come from, Aris could see no one. It was the same voice he'd heard the day his dad was sick. It was at that moment the lift doors opened.

Aris strained his eyes. From his position at the other end of the corridor, it appeared there was a woman stood just inside the lift. She wore a long white dress, tainted with green stains and soaked right through.

"Come, Aris. Run!" the woman shouted. She was far away but Aris heard her clearly.

He tentatively walked down the hallway towards her. And the closer he got to the lift, the more she faded from his vision. His pace quickened as the woman spoke out again, "Run."

Aris soon reached the elevator and, as he stepped in, he could no longer see the woman, except a dwindling outline of her against the large mirror that stretched the whole of the lift. He stepped in and placed his hand against the hard surface of the mirror, a chill raced down his spine.

At that exact moment, the lift closed. He turned to see four men dressed in dark suits, with the technological glasses, come up from the stairway. The lift doors shut, and the button light flashed for the basement. Aris descended.

Reaching the bottom, the lift opened. Aris stepped out into the basement. It was dark and quiet.

"Hello?" Aris said as he made his way into the corridor.

He looked around for the lady, but he couldn't see her. *What's happening? Who is she?* He couldn't help but remember the strange things he used to see when he was younger. The visions and daydreams he used to have so often. They were so frequent back then, before his mum passed away.

As Aris neared the entrance to the stairwell, he felt a strange sensation, like he was being watched. He twisted around, searching for someone, but again, no one was there. As he brought his attention back to the stairwell, he stopped. Looming over him was a man in a dark suit. Aris glanced down to the man's hand. He held a strange baton, which had intricate patterns etched onto it.

Aris stepped backwards, raising his hands. The man rapidly brought the baton high and aimed it at Aris. Without warning, Aris launched a kick. Surprisingly, his foot hit the baton, which flew into the air. The man immediately punched Aris in the face, sending him smashing to the ground.

As Aris hit the floor, he heard a loud *snap*, and the sensation of pouring water drenched his face. He cocked his head to see the man pick up the baton from behind him.

Aris cradled his face with his hands. It throbbed. He wiped away some of the blood and could feel a large chunk of his left nostril had been ripped off. The skin clung to his face.

Aris lifted himself up and scrambled towards the elevator. The doors were open as he stumbled in. He looked back to see that the man was being joined by two others.

Aris frantically pressed the lift button door to shut, but it didn't. In that moment, he glanced up at the lift mirror. In the distance, he was astonished to see someone running towards him. Squinting to focus through his blurry vision, Aris could see Professor Maxwell, but only in the reflection of the mirror, on turning to face the corridor he only saw the three men.

Returning his gaze back to the mirror, he was flabbergasted to see Pep race past the men and continue towards Aris in the lift. As the image of the professor came closer, Aris could see the professor enter the lift, but only in the reflection.

It was at this moment that the professor reached the mirror, and to Aris's shock, Pep flew out of the mirror and into the lift. He flipped through the air and rolled out into the corridor. Aris couldn't quite believe what he was seeing. The professor had literally come out of the mirror and into reality before his very eyes.

The three advancing men, were now close to the professor, too. They were equally as perplexed as Aris was. They couldn't quite believe what they'd just witnessed, until one of them shrieked, "It's a fucking Seecher!"

The three of them raised their batons. In one quick motion, Pep waved his hands through the air, and an invisible force slammed the men against the left wall of the hallway before sending them back against the opposite wall. As each of them lost grip of their batons, they were lifted high and slammed into the ceiling, where they remained fixed and lifeless.

The professor returned to the lift and grabbed Aris.

"Stay with me Aris. You're losing a lot of blood," the professor said as he steadied Aris up to his feet. Pep turned and waved his hand in the air, as if reading it with his palms.

"There's far more of them coming. You have to come with me. We need to move fast," Pep said as he took out a small blue, glowing circle on his necklace from underneath his clothing. Brilliant light illuminated the lift. The professor moved towards the mirror, aimed the glowing circle and flung some of its shimmering contents against it. As drops of blue glowing liquid hit the mirror, it rippled out like stones cast in a river. Aris turned and stared. His reflection wrinkled and flexed as it became fluid, like the surface of a waterfall.

"What the hell?" Aris whispered as his eyes widened.

"It's our means of escape, Aris. It's called the Oneiri," the professor said as he pulled Aris close, and they walked straight through the rippling liquid reflection.

CHAPTER FIVE

FIVE WHAT?

As soon as Pep and Aris had passed through the threshold, the three suited men held against the ceiling plummeted to the ground. The lift was now empty, but to Aris, it seemed as if they'd walked forward through the mirror, only to step back into the same lift again.

He could hear Pep talking to him as he was helped from the lift, but the words were too faint to hear. The pain in Aris's nose was too intense for him to concentrate, and he could feel himself slowly passing out.

"We have to move quickly," Pep commanded as he steered Aris along the corridor.

Aris felt his body become weaker. In a few more seconds, he crashed to the floor.

"Tyche," Pep said.

At that moment, the room filled with a coloured haze. The professor scooped up a handful of sapphire fog, moulded it in his hands, and then placed it against Aris's face. A grotesque cracking sound rang out. Aris's pain subsided, but his eyes became heavy, and they closed as he lost consciousness.

"Sleep, gather your energies," the professor said as he picked Aris up.

Around them, many more men in dark suits flooded into the corridor. Not one of them could see Pep walk off with Aris in his arms. Each gave a shudder as the Seecher and Aris, passed straight through them.

Adam sat drinking a glass of red wine. The overcooked joint of beef he'd roasted two hours ago now lay cold on the kitchen side. He glanced down at the time on his watch. It was past nine o'clock.

Maya unlocked the front door and entered the house.

"Maya?" her father shouted.

She didn't respond. She walked slowly toward her dad, who stood at the dining room table.

"Tulip, are you okay? Where have you been?" Adam said as he examined her troubled face.

Maya stared him right in the eyes. She let go of the bag in her left hand but continued to tightly grip the book in her right.

"Maya, what's the matter?" Adam asked, coming closer.

There was a moment of unnerving silence. Adam scrunched his eyes.

"Why didn't you tell me?"

"Tell you what?" Adam shook his head.

"That you're a Seecher!"

"What?" Adam replied. "I don't know what you're talking about, Maya. What's this about?"

"Don't lie to me," Maya screamed as she launched the book at her father's chest.

It slammed hard into him. He didn't flinch, even though the force of it had been enough to hurt. He watched as the book tumbled to the floor and opened to a random page. His eyes widened as memories flooded back. He could make out the handwriting that covered the pages. The scribbles belonged to his dead wife, Monica.

He looked up slowly at his daughter. "How did you get that?"

"That's it? That's all you've got to say? How did I get it?! How did I find mum's private journal? That's so meaningless. It's not how I got it that matters?! What matters is that you've lied to me. No, you've lied to me my whole life. Now, tell me, are you a Seecher or not?" Her voice came out jagged and sharp.

Adam bent down and picked up the notebook, as if it were a newborn baby. Involuntary tears rolled down his cheeks.

"Answer me!" Maya howled, but her father's head stayed bowed.

"A Seecher?" he whispered.

"Are you one? Tell me!" she pleaded, her eyes also begun to fill with tears.

Adam stood up with the book.

"Yes."

"Yes. Say the words," Maya bawled.

"I am a Seecher. How on earth did you find this out? Is it written in Monica's book? Is that how?"

"A bit from there, but more from a perceptive friend," Maya breathed out as she made her way to the table and took a seat. Her father sat on the chair in front of her, placing the book down.

"By friend, do you mean that boy?"

She eyed her dad but ignored his question. "Why haven't you told me?"

"I didn't tell you to protect you."

"Protect me? From what?"

"It's difficult to explain, Maya."

"Try."

"It's dangerous knowledge. I needed to keep you safe from it."

"Safe from what, Dad?" she barked back.

"What do you know about the Seechers? Do you know what it means to be one?"

"I know a fair bit."

"You know that a Seecher studies the Great Mystery."

"I know there's been many great people in the past who've studied the Great Mystery, and by studying it, you obtain great knowledge and power."

"That's kind of true. Do you know the old adage, Absolute power corrupts absolutely? Or at least it has the potential to."

"You didn't tell me because you were trying to protect me from becoming corrupt?" Maya asked, not waiting for a response. "What a pile of shit!" She stood up in defiance.

"Maya, please, sit down. That is true. I only ever wanted to keep you safe from a dangerous world filled with turmoil and pain. Everything I did has been to protect you. You must believe that," Adam implored as he too stood up.

"I don't care what your intentions are, you've lied. You kept details about your life, my life, from me. Was Mum a Seecher, too?" Maya said.

"She was. Yes."

Maya stumbled back.

"Why?" Maya cried. "Why did you hide this from me? I hate you!"

"Maya, please, I wanted to tell you, I did, but I couldn't. I swear I was just sparing you from heartache." Adam stepped closer to her, but she recoiled.

"Don't touch me! You've completely deceived me, and I'll never forgive you for this. I don't even know what you do anymore! All those times you've said you're going to work, all the business trips, here I am thinking you're off working with your sales team, but you're not, are you?!" Maya broke down.

"No. Sorry."

"You've kept everything about mum away from me. You've kept her all locked away to yourself. You're a selfish fucking monster, and I hate you." Tears raced down her face as she stepped away from her father.

"I never meant to keep her from you, but I had to avoid you learning anything about the Seechers. I'm under oath not to tell anyone about it, and that includes you."

"I don't care! Your life is one big fat lie. A big fucking joke. You're not at all who you say you are. No wonder you're so alone. I really hate you for this. I wish it was you who had died instead of mum," Maya screamed, picking up his wine glass on the side and smashing it to the floor.

"At least if it had been you instead of mum, I would still have one parent and the memory of the other. With you, all I've had is a faceless shadow. You're an empty, hollow man who's done nothing but lie to me," Maya shouted.

"You don't know what you're talking about. You know nothing of the burden I bear."

"You've ruined my life. Bear that!" Maya barked as she made her way for the door, "I wish it had been you."

"How dare you speak to me like that?! Don't you walk out. You want to know?! Let's talk, Maya. You bloody want to know all the horrible things that have happened?! You're such a big girl now, you don't need protecting? Is that it?!" Adam shouted as he followed Maya into the hallway.

"Fuck you. You're not my dad anymore."

"Maya! Parents deceive their children all the time to keep them safe. To lessen the pain. You'll find that out yourself one day. See how you feel then. If I'm guilty of anything, it's that. Lying to protect you. You wish it was me that died instead of your mother? Well, guess what, so do I. But it wasn't. Fate didn't work out that way. You want the truth, Maya? You want the bastard truth?!"

"Leave me alone." Maya trembled as she held the door handle.

"Your mother left us, Maya. She left us. She couldn't handle it, and she left us."

"Do you mean she's alive?" Maya turned and whispered.

"No. She killed herself."

"You're lying. She died in a car crash. You told me she died in a crash on the Albert Bridge on 3 March, 1999 at 11:18pm, from a collision with a speeding lorry," Maya sobbed.

"I couldn't tell you what really happened."

"Why?!" Maya bellowed.

"Because I couldn't bring myself to say it aloud. I've always planned to tell you the truth when you were old enough to understand it. But as each year passes, it gets harder to say. That's why I've kept it from you. I'm sorry I've had to tell you like this."

"Why would she kill herself?" Maya's words were barely audible through her tears.

"Maya, the study of absolute power can corrupt absolutely. Becoming a Seecher tainted your mother. She was a lot like you, determined, smart…forthright…obsessive. The search for greater knowledge consumed her. It warped her. To the point where it was all too much. Becoming a Seecher's not an undertaking that comes without huge cost." As he finished, he leant in to comfort her. She let him rest his arm on her shoulder for a moment.

"You should have told me."

"I'm sorry. I tried. I just…I just couldn't."

"You haven't explained anything. You're just hiding behind a screen of lies, hoping no one sees you. How does it feel when you've lied so much you can't even tell the difference between what's true and what's not?" Maya pushed off his hand as she twisted the door handle and opened the door. "How do you expect me to trust anything you say?"

———

A slim, athletic woman with dark hair and an East-Asian complexion walked into a long, narrow room. Her name was Kathryn Winton, though everyone called her Kat. She was in her thirties and had been a Seecher for over a decade. The room she had walked into was impressive, adorned with intricately-carved patterns made up of ancient symbols and texts, which stretched across the stone walls and covered the ceilings.

At the centre of the room sat Pep in a hooded gown. He was alone, at a circular table, with six seats around it. Even the table and chairs had complex designs and ciphers etched into them.

"Kat. You're early," said Pep as he looked up from his meditative state.

"I'm early, or everyone else is late." Kat smiled.

"Sel's out. He'll be back any minute. Tallia's with Aris, making sure I didn't botch the job I did of fixing his nose," Pep replied.

"And Adam?" Kat enquired.

"He'll be with us tomorrow."

"Why did you need to fix his nose? Was it broken? Was he attacked?" Kat asked as she took a seat.

"Yes. There were several men who were armed with weapons of the old enemy," Pep said.

"The Tauredunum Raiders?!" Kat exclaimed. Pep nodded. "Have you told the other Elders?"

"Sel's prepared a message for them, detailing our findings."

"Have you confirmed it then? That the disappearances and the attackers are linked?" Kat asked as the door behind her opened.

"It's what we're advising the Guild Elders. After what I saw, it's eminently clear that's the case," Pep finished, and they both turned their attention to Selwyn Adjei, the forty-five-year-old man who'd just entered the room.

He marched forwards with purpose, tall and broad. His dark

complexion hinted to his Ghanaian heritage, although his accent was well-spoken English.

"The last of the Potentials are here and settled. They're asking a lot of questions, naturally. The only one not to join them yet is Aris," Sel said as he took a seat next to Kat.

"He's still in medical with Tallia," Pep confirmed.

"Has anyone else been attacked?" Kat asked.

"No, just Aris. It was fortunate I arrived when I did. The attackers would have killed him. It's still not clear to me why they were after him and what they want with our Potentials. There wasn't a trace of anything when I returned. We still have nothing," said Pep.

"How have the Tauredunum returned? After all this time?" Sel gestured with his hands.

"I thought they'd all died, a long time ago," Kat asked Pep.

"Just because it's Tauredunum technology they're using doesn't mean they're necessarily the original Tauredunum Raiders," Pep answered.

"Well, it explains why we're finding it so difficult to trace who they are. Tauredunum technology's infamous for being designed so Seechers cannot detect it," Sel continued.

"Maybe that's why they want the Potentials," Kat said, as she sat in a momentary trance, holding her head in her hands.

"You know what, Kat. You could be right." Sel said as he pointed his finger in the air.

"Explain," Pep encouraged.

"Well, the original Tauredunum technology was powered by stolen Epsilon from the Seechers which, because it was tampered with it became corrupted. I remember reading an account that described how the Tauredunum methods, sometimes produced a contaminated version of Epsilon, one they called Epsilac. It was described as a dull yellow, quarter-life version of Epsilon. It was unreliable, weapons powered by the Epsilac would often malfunction. Hence their failed efforts at extraction. There's a small sample of it in the Alcaios archive in Tibet where I was did my Alcaios warrior training, I was shown it." Sel put his arms behind his head as he leaned back into his chair.

"There's a reference to Epsilac in the older archives around the development of the original activation techniques. It didn't describe it like Sel just did, but it did say that failed activation techniques would produce weak Epsilon, comparable to the Tauredunum Epsilac. I didn't know at the time when I read it that Epsilac could be so different." Kat paused for a moment as she shared an ominous look with Sel. "What if the strange attackers are trying to forcibly harvest Epsilon from Potentials? They might at least cultivate Epsilac," Kat wondered.

"I'm not sure if that's even possible." Sel sat back up.

"But with today's technology, I wouldn't be surprised if it was. It would support some of the visions I have been having. Those about the hospital wards and that strange menacing machine." Kat uttered as she shook her head.

"This will need to be recorded for the Elders to review," Pep said to Sel, who stood up.

"I'll go and add that now."

"No, wait one minute, we're not done here," Pep instructed.

Kat had sort of woken herself up out of her trance, then randomly asked, "Are you going to speak to the Potentials now? What are you going to tell them?"

"When Aris's awake, I'll explain as much as possible." Pep nodded.

"If we have any Nous Potentials, I bet they'll have already dreamt about the others being attacked. You know how close batches of Potentials can be. Even when they've never met each other," Kat chirped.

Pep took this in. "Yes, that's true. It's such a long time since the last cycle. One forgets."

Sel tried to push this along. "It's only seven years. I guess we'll find out when we talk to them."

Pep wasn't ready to end their meeting just yet.

"What have you said to yours?" Pep asked.

"Some bits. Nothing too heavy," Kat replied.

"And you, Sel?"

"I've told them what I needed to, so they came with me here. They're all a little frightened. It's understandable. I've assured them they'll come to no harm. It always amazes me how much students trust their teachers." Sel smiled at Pep.

Before Pep could enquire further, Tallia walked in.

"He's awake," she announced.

Pep got up and followed Tallia back out of the room and headed for Aris. Sel and Kat followed them out. Kat peeled off to go and prepare the Potentials for Pep, and Sel went to update the message to the Elders.

Aris lay on an examination bed in a room full of medical equipment, some items conventional and recognizable, others were not. Pep and Tallia entered.

"Professor." Aris tried to sit up as much as he could.

"How are you feeling?" Pep asked.

"Like I'm dreaming." The two Seechers had a little chuckle. Aris touched his nose. "I thought my nose was broken. Ouch."

"It was. But we've fixed it. It's a little bruised still," Pep said as he walked towards Aris. Tallia followed closely.

"How can you fix a broken nose that quickly? Is this some kind of magic?" Aris asked. They both smiled.

"No, Aris. To answer that fully, you're going to have to trust me," Pep said as he sat on the bed. "This is my companion, Tallia." She smiled and softly said, "Hello."

Aris was quick to respond. "You're Seechers, right?"

"We are. I'm impressed you even know that word. How have you come across this term?" Pep asked.

"I've done my homework." Pep raised an eyebrow, and Aris continued, "You're gonna have to trust me on that one."

"Trust is of upmost importance right now. I'm willing to tell you all you need to know about the Seechers. What we are. What we do. Why we exist. But when I do, you have to promise me one thing," requested Pep.

"Promise you what?"

"That with everything you're told and shown here, you witness it with an open and willing mind," Pep said.

Aris agreed, "Sure." He even stretched out his hand, which Pep kindly shook.

"Do you know if my dad's okay?" Aris asked.

"Your dad's safe and well," Pep nodded.

Aris leant forwards. "How do you know that?"

"Because I went back and checked. He's still in the hospital, in safe hands."

"Thank you," Aris said as he sat up further, dropping his legs to the ground.

"Do you have any idea why those men were after you? And how they knew of your whereabouts?" Tallia asked.

"No. But I've dreamt of them. Who are they? What do they want?" Aris frowned.

"Unfortunately, we don't have all the answers right now. But when we do, we'll share it with you," Tallia replied.

"I haven't thanked you for saving me." Aris stood up.

"No need. I'm glad you're safe. Now, if you're up to it, I'd like to show you the first revelation," Pep said.

Tallia and Pep directed Aris to a large sitting area, filled with lots of young people. At first, he didn't recognize anyone until his eyes fell on three faces that made him instantly feel at ease.

Leo, Abi and Thomas all saw Aris at the same time and rushed towards him.

"Aris. This is mental. Are you okay? Crap, your nose. Ohhh," Leo said as he moved in and gave him a manly embrace.

"We heard you were attacked?" Thomas said.

"That's why Pep brought us here," Abi confirmed.

"I'm much better for seeing you guys. Fuck, this is so epically weird. I don't even know how to start to tell you how crazy this is," Aris replied, leaning in for a group hug.

"Don't worry, man, we're here for you," Leo reassured him.

Aris looked up at Thomas. "You're never gonna believe this..."

"What?" Thomas asked.

Aris continued, "The men who attacked me, remember the dreams we both had?"

Thomas looked at him concerned. "The men with the rods."

"Oh, damn. Don't tell me it was them?!" Abi tried to control herself as Aris nodded at them.

"Ah, man, this is getting way too spooky. Are you sure?" Abi asked, hopping on the spot.

"Hundred percent," Aris replied.

Before any of them could extend their conversation further, the professor stepped forward and spoke loudly for all to hear.

"Can I have everyone's attention, please? My name's Pep Maxwell, some of you will have met me before, others of you may not have. But you'll at least be familiar with one of my companions who's brought you here tonight. You're no doubt filled with many questions, and we'll answer as many as possible. But first, it's important I give all of you an overall understanding of why we've had to bring you here with such urgency. Which for the most part, is for your own safety."

Pep looked around at the fifteen fresh young faces that stared wide-eyed back at him.

"I wish not to alarm you, but for the time being, we highly recommend you make appropriate excuses as to where you are, and you remain here for the next few days, until we've put a stop to these attacks on you young people." The room fell silent.

Kat stepped in. "We have already lost many like you. Some of them you may be aware of, others none of you will know about. Those among you who may one day become Nous Seechers, will have already seen these attacks in your dreams." Abi, Thomas, and Aris all looked at each other. Their jaws dropped.

"Does anyone want to raise their hand if you've experienced this?" Aris and Thomas raised their hands and were surprised to see two others raise their hands, too. "Right. That's because, Potential Seechers are a lot more connected to one another than you understand at the moment. It's not uncommon for Potential Seechers to have dreams of this nature. If you have had anything like this, it is a good indicator you're a Potential, and is nothing to fear," Kat finished and took a step down.

Pep nodded to her as he continued. Thomas had a second to turn to Abi and whisper, "What the fuck's a Nous Seecher?" Abi had no option but to shrug as they both turned to listen to what Pep had to say.

"You're here becuase you are all extremely gifted individuals. Some of the most exquisitely imaginative, intelligent, and creative minds of your generation, here in the UK." A little discussion, mainly flattered excitement, buzzed in the room. "This makes you highly sought after by competing employers, yes. But clearly also by these dangerous people who have started attacking Potentials. They want something you don't even know that you have." There was a brief murmur.

"What makes you so intelligent?" Pep asked over the din. A few suggestions came from the small crowd. Learning. Language. Empathy. Discipline. Contemplation.

"No," Pep said, "it is a very powerful substance that is inside your brain, it's called Epsilon, that you all have a lot of. Some of you more than others, but everyone here will have much more than the average person. This is what our attackers are after." Chatter filled the room.

"Now, had the attacks not taken place, at some point next year, we would have brought you here, anyway. So, to keep this positive we will discuss what we would be saying if none of this awful business had started. Because here, in the Seecher Guild, there is an amazing opportunity for some of you. Because some of you, not all, but some, will have the potential to become Seechers. And before you all start asking me what a Seecher is, I shall start to answer that with this. A Seecher is someone who has unlocked the full ability of their subconscious mind. They have gained access to a great knowledge, and from that knowledge comes great power. This all may seem farfetched and fantastical. But I can promise you, that what we show you, is the truth. The ultimate truth, that underpins all of existence." Pep beamed.

"It's not something I've made up. It has been understood and practiced for nearly three thousand years…the Seechers have existed for millennia, but the world at large is unaware. We have kept it hidden, guarded it. Because this knowledge can be hugely dangerous, and in the wrong hands, it could prove to be the undoing of all life on Earth."

He paused to let the gravity of his words sink in.

"Like you, thirty odd years ago, my lecturer brought me and my friends to this exact room and I first learnt of the Seechers, and it takes time and effort and concentration, to ever fully understand what Seechers are. So, be patient with yourselves and with us, and we will embark on this epic adventure together. One step at a time."

Pep took a deep breath as he started to bring his speech to a close.

"Sel, Kat, Tallia, and I will spend the next few hours answering individual questions. But before that begins, there are three things I need to say. Number one, no question you ask is silly or off-limits. Number two, you will be faced with two choices soon. It is completely up to you to decide whether to take the examination to see if you are a Potential or not. We cannot tell for sure, without the test. The test tells us if you possess the ability to become a Seecher. Third, and finally, if you take the test and pass, you and you alone, will decide whether to undergo the Seecher trials and the activation ceremony. If you complete these steps, you will join us as a Seecher," Pep finished, and as he signalled for questions, hands were raised. Every single person had a question.

Aris had many questions, but he held back a while as he sat and listened to the others enquire on what being a Seecher meant — they all seemed to agree that, although intriguing, the professor's speech had been a bit opaque. They questioned what the test involved and what happens in the activation ceremony. The general answers given remained somewhat frustratingly mystical. Nearly an hour had passed, and the group had broken off into smaller ones. The four Seechers started to mingle around the room, offering more focused answers and insights.

Aris stood with Thomas, Abi and Leo as Tallia made her way over.

"Are you four okay? Any questions for me?" she asked.

Thomas was quick to ask specifics on what the *great knowledge* was. Aris listened as Tallia described how our minds are limited by our perception and that when an individual undergoes the activation, they gain a Key that grants them access to seeing the universe around them in a vastly different way. Aris couldn't help but feel that her response was a little vague and was surprised to see Thomas accepting the answer so readily.

Maya wouldn't be so easily placated, Aris thought. As that consideration entered his mind, it was soon followed by, *Where is Maya? If there was anyone who was possibly one of these Seecher Potentials, it was surely her.*

He completely ignored the group and made his way to Pep.

"Where's Maya? Why isn't she here?" Aris asked.

"That's complicated, Aris. There's a lot I'm willing to share with you.

But to divulge the reason why Maya isn't here, why she's not to be considered as a Potential, is something I cannot offer, as it would mean breaking a bond I have with a very dear friend," Pep replied.

"Fine. I get that. But her dad is a Seecher, right, as was her mother?" Aris asked.

"Yes, he is, and she once was, too, yes. I'm impressed you know all that. How do you know this?" Pep asked, frowning, "Does Maya know this?"

"Yes. I told her," Aris replied as Pep's face drained of colour.

"Excuse me, please," Pep said as he walked off and whispered something in Tallia's ear.

***

"Hello," Adam answered his phone. "Yeah, I know, Tallia. We've just been talking about it. I told her. I had no other choice." Adam paused, wiping a fresh tear from his eye as he listened to Tallia's response. "No, I don't need anything. Just time. Thank you, no, I don't need you to come over, this is a family matter, and I wish to keep it that way. I need time to sort this out. Maya's in a fragile state and, quite frankly, so am I… Tell Pep I have to focus on Maya right now, not to expect me in any time soon." Adam ended the call. He made his way up the stairs, into his bedroom. Inside, there was a large mirror that adorned the length of the entire wall. He took his phone out of his pocket, turned it off, and placed it in his bedside table drawer.

Adam then took out his Seecher Key, a glowing blue Klein bottle, that was kept hidden inside his shirt. The circular shaped bottle itself was identical to the one Pep wore, but the design of the necklace was personalized. Adam flicked some of the blue glowing Epsilon onto the mirror and watched as it turned the solid material into rippling fluid. He then stepped through and entered the Oneiri.

Adam searched the university library, the local coffee shops, the student union bar, all inside the Oneiri. There was no sign of Maya anywhere. Adam knew if she wasn't at home and wasn't at uni, there was only one other place she could be. Her internship. Despite only being there a few months, she seemed to love the place, especially the library.

It wasn't long before Adam was standing outside the Curative Analytical building. People walked straight through him, invisible to all those around him. That was one of the many advantages of the Oneiri. Adam waited for someone to enter the main reception and quickly followed behind them. Unknown to him, a small glass vial that rested inside the wall glowed a dull yellow at the exact moment he crossed the threshold to the building. The glass vial was connected to a stream of electric wiring snaking around the building. Since the system's creation, they had never been activated before.

Adam continued his search around the building, completely unaware that, as he crossed invisible barriers, these small glass objects within the walls glowed, and that this had tripped an unused and untested internal top security system.

Dr Rivers raced to the security room. Simon was already there monitoring a security screen, which had a schematic plan of the building displayed whilst a series of yellow dots blinked *on*. As Dr Rivers watched, a new yellow dot appeared just a little ahead of the last.

"There," Simon pointed at the screen.

"Amazing. It's one of them." Dr Rivers's face filled with glee. "What does the CCTV show?"

Simon pointed at another screen. Dr Rivers quickly scanned the feed from the hallway. There was nothing. No one, no movement on the screen, just an empty corridor.

A new yellow dot shone brightly.

"This is it. Open all the doorways to the snare. Lead them to it. Prepare all agents. I want the security level completely locked down," Dr Rivers ordered one of the agents standing behind him, who was to carry out the task.

Simon typed away on a keyboard next to him, moments later symbols on the screen changed, to show a number of doors were no longer locked. Simon systematically opened a series of doors which led straight up to level nine. The security level and to one specific room.

The two men watched eagerly as more yellow dots traced across the screen all flowing in the direction of the pathway Simon had created. They continued to watch the screen with great anticipation, and it wasn't long before the yellow dots made their way to a space, which on the screen was entitled The Snare Room.

———

The path Adam had taken had been completely unobstructed. He'd not found the library, but he'd become increasingly curious as to what exactly went on in this building. There were many signs and door names that possibly indicated the nature of the work was ominously similar to that of the Seechers.

He carried on his fortuitously clear path. His search for Maya was now taking second place to a new quest for any information on who precisely Maya was working for. As he turned a corridor, he could see a long row of rooms. Walking passed each one, he tried the handles, but they were all locked. Whilst he was inside the Oneiri, it would have been extremely difficult to open them, even if they weren't locked, and practically impossible since they were.

He tried a few more doors, but they were also locked. Looking up, his attention was drawn to a room at the end. The door was ajar, but what piqued his curiosity was the plaque that rested above the entrance. It bore one word: *Nihilo.*

Adam moved towards the room. He pushed the door, it was heavy to him in the Oneiri, he strained to finally open it wide, and then crept inside. The room itself was probably about three meters long and three meters wide. The floor was bare, and the room empty, except for one strangely familiar element. Every wall, including the rear of the door, was mirrored.

Adam looked around in wonder. Suddenly, he jumped in shock. The door he'd just entered through slammed shut. It thumped hard, mechanical workings hidden away locked it tightly in its frame. Adam leapt to the door and tried to turn the handle. It moved slightly. He strained with every fibre of his being, every ounce of his energy, but all he managed was a slight wiggle. He was trapped.

———

Simon had pressed the button to lock the doors on Dr Rivers's command, as soon as one of the dots had appeared on the screen in the 'Snare Room'.

"Reset the sensors along this path, if it escapes, I want to know," Dr Rivers growled his orders as he turned his attention back to the live video feed on the split screen. One showed the outer door, the other displayed the interior of the *Snare Room*.

After a few seconds, Dr Rivers was filled with delight as his eyes caught a glimpse of motion on the external feed. It was the outside door handle. He watched as it twisted and jiggled ever so slightly.

"We did it. We've actually caught a Seecher," Dr Rivers exclaimed as he stood up straight. "Have agents stationed outside that door. Prepare the flooring. Call everyone in," he barked, his eyes fixated on the screen.

Maya had walked the streets of London under the pale moonlight for nearly three hours. Her mindless amble finished when she could no longer emotionally tolerate going over the same thoughts anymore. Her face was covered by the dried-out traces of her tears. She walked through her front door, tentatively making her way into the main living area, expecting to see her father waiting and ready to reconcile.

Maya looked around the house, but there was no sign of her dad anywhere. She called out for him, but there was no reply. She suspected he might have gone to bed, but on checking his room, it was empty. It wasn't a complete surprise he wasn't there. He would often leave her in the house alone. She concluded he must have headed off for his trip early.

She ended up on her bed, phone in hand. She was going to call him, to apologize, but decided not to. She texted her dad a simple message.

- I am sorry for what I said. When you're back, please, can we talk? I love you.

Maya watched as it sent. She waited, staring at the screen for a few minutes, waiting for the *read* icon to appear. After five minutes, she closed the app and tried to call Aris.

Aris's dreams had been filled with all sorts of mesmerizing confusion. Dream after dream about what a Seecher might be and who Pep really was. He didn't wake in-between the dreams, they seamlessly flowed from one to the next. The most recurrent dream that had plagued him for some time now, played out again. A rooftop edge. Maya holding a gun. As the gun fired. Aris bolted awake.

Looking around the unfamiliar room Aris felt disorientated in his new surroundings. The room was very foreign from anything Aris had ever seen before, let alone slept in. He looked over and saw several beds, and then instantly remembered he was in the Seechers building. He turned to his side and could see Leo fast asleep in the bed next to him.

Aris glanced at his watch. It was six o'clock in the morning. He remembered Pep had told them that they would be up at seven to begin the testing sessions, to see if they were what he called *Potentials*. He then reached down and picked up his phone. He only had 15% of battery left, and to save it, he'd turned the phone onto airplane mode. As he switched the airplane mode off, his phone instantly lit up as he received seven texts from Maya, and then noticed he had five missed calls throughout the night.

Aris got up, quickly dressed, and crept out of the room. The entire building was quiet. He stealthily made his way to what he guessed was the exit.

As he navigated a long corridor, he became unsure whether he was heading in the right direction or not. When it came to an end, he could see a strange metal door. He tentatively pushed against it. It swung open. Aris stepped through and found himself in the middle of a London tube station. He quickly looked back at the door, but the door had gone. There was nothing there but the small white tiles that made up the wall. The door had completely vanished.

"What the hell?" Aris couldn't believe it. He stood there, open-mouthed. *How will I ever know to come back here?* he thought. He put his hands into his pockets and took out a pen. He then drew a circle and an X inside on one of the tiles. He took a step back to admire his work, then shrugged and sprinted off.

It was just before seven that Aris arrived. Knocking and ringing the bell, Maya answered.

"Aris. What's happened to your face?" Maya yawned.

"Oh that. Don't worry. Are you okay? Maya, what's happened?" he asked as he stood on the doorstep.

"Come in," she said, ignoring his questions.

Aris walked in and followed Maya as she dragged herself to the lounge and fell onto the sofa.

"So...what happened?" Aris asked as he sat down.

"I was a bit melodramatic last night. Sorry for all my ranting messages. I've slept on it now, and I'm feeling a lot better," Maya replied, curling up in a ball.

"You're telling me you slept?" Aris said as he looked her up and down.

"I'm good," she replied, closing her eyes.

"How did it go with your dad?" Aris said, giving her legs a shake.

"Well, I asked him outright. And then it all went horribly, horribly wrong," Maya said, putting her hands to her face.

"What did he say? What went wrong?"

"I asked him if he was a Seecher, and the conversation then moved on to my mum. He talked about her more in one night than he's done my entire life. We argued a lot. He told me things I didn't know. I got super angry and stormed out." As Maya spoke, she fidgeted, sitting up again.

"What did he say that you didn't know? Did he admit he's a Seecher?"

"Yes, he admitted it but didn't say much about it. And then he told me about how my mum died. He told me she hadn't died in an accident as I was led to believe, but that she...she killed herself...because she couldn't handle being a Seecher, that she was *tainted*. That's when I got angry and left. Then when I got back home, he'd already gone," Maya said, turning to Aris.

"Wow. Bloody hell. Is that true?"

"God knows what's true?" Maya groaned.

"Maya, I'm so sorry I didn't pick up my phone last night. I should have been there for you," Aris said as he placed a hand on top of hers.

She smiled at him before she continued, "It's okay. I can't expect you to be there all the time."

"I should have been."

"It's fine, Aris. I'm a big girl. I'll survive this." She paused briefly. "Is your dad okay?"

"Yeah, I called the hospital this morning. He's still there, but he's okay. Mrs Potter, our neighbour, is going to visit him this afternoon." There was a long pause.

"Why's your nose bruised?" she asked as Aris raised an eyebrow.

"Shit, Maya. I had the strangest night of my life last night. But to be honest, with everything you've just gone through, I'm not sure now's the right time to tell you."

"Stop being a douche and tell me." Maya leant in.

"Fine, but don't get angry with me." Aris stopped as Maya scowled. He quickly continued. "Okay! After you left me last night at the hospital, I was attacked."

"What the fuck? By who?" Maya jumped up out of her seat and paced around.

"I was attacked by these men in the hospital. The men Thomas and I both had dreams about."

"What?!"

"They just appeared out of nowhere. I tried to get away. I kicked a rod out of a guy's hand, and then he punched me in the nose."

"How did you escape?!"

"Pep came to my rescue."

"Pep?! So, he is keeping an eye on you. What did he do? Call the police?"

"No, no, nothing of the sort, Maya. He came out of the mirror and, like, kicked their butts, and then he healed my nose. It was practically falling off, then he took me back to the Seecher Guild, and that's where I stayed last night. I've just come from there."

"Are you for real? You're pulling my leg, right? If this is a joke, Aris, you're seriously not funny," Maya said, jumping about on the spot.

"I probably shouldn't tell you the rest."

"The rest?! You've told me everything so far? What can't you tell me?"

"Well, I'm sure I've been sworn into some sort of secrecy, but we started this adventure together, and we'll end it together. You're in my dreams, for fuck's sake," Aris muttered.

"What?" Maya frowned.

"Nothing," Aris replied. "Okay, when Pep rescued me from the attackers in the hospital, I was out of it. Then I woke up in the Seechers building. Pep then told me that he's a Seecher."

"Wow! Okay, I get it. Shit. Right. Carry on. Carry on," Maya screeched with excitement.

"There were about fifteen others there."

"Other Seechers?"

"No. Young people like us."

"Oh, why was that?"

"Leo, Abi and Thomas were also there."

"What?!"

"Yeah. They're still there. They'd brought them all in because I'd been attacked, and they were worried about everyone's safety. Then Pep told us, all of us, that we could be Seechers if we want to. Well, if we pass their test. Then we can decide."

"Get the fuck out of here?! You can't be serious. Aris! You're on the inside now. You've done it! Oh, my fucking God, I've been trying to uncover this Seecher business for three years, and in just a month you've waltzed right into the belly of the beast!" Maya sat back next to him.

"So, what is a Seecher then? What do they do? Did they mention my dad? Where's their building? How did you get out? How do I get in?" Aris took her hands.

"I don't really know. They were pretty vague about everything. They kind of implied they have some great knowledge, an understanding of the universe that would bring enlightenment or something. It was all rather culty, if you ask me. I don't really know what they do, something about following a code. I did ask Pep if your dad was a Seecher and why you weren't there, too. He has a promise with your dad, I think, to keep you out of it."

"What the hell! So, every one of my best friends are going to become Seechers and I'm not?" She stood up again.

"I'm not doing this without you, Maya. You're the reason I'm buried deep in this crap in the first place!" Aris smiled at Maya.

"You need to find your way back in. Gather as much information as you can. I'll work on my dad." Maya nodded.

"Maya, there is something else. I keep having this dream."

"What dream?"

"We're on top of some really tall building, and I'm holding something you really want. You demand I give it back to you, but I don't. I can't. And then…you shoot me."

"Ha! With what?"

"A gun."

"I have a gun, and I shoot you?" Maya stood back up, pacing.

"Yes."

"Is this a dream that glimpses into the future?"

"I don't know. But it keeps happening."

"Aris. I would never shoot you. Not in a million years. Not ever."

CHAPTER SIX

The Final Piece

Aris found his way back to the tube station and the wall where, a few hours earlier, he had left the Seechers building. He knew he was back at same spot, as his drawing of the X in the circle was still there. He wandered along the tunnel, and when he was sure he was alone, he frantically searched the wall for any sign of a door or an opening. He was unsuccessful.

Nearly twenty minutes went by as Aris examined the tiles where he believed the entrance was. He was about to give up and head back to Maya's when a voice bellowed out, "You're late."

Pep's face was stern, though there was a hint of mischief in his eyes.

"I'm really sorry," Aris muttered.

"Sorry for absconding in the early hours of the morning? Or sorry you're late for the Potential's testing?" Pep ask as he manoeuvred around Aris and rested against the wall.

"Both? I guess." Aris shrugged.

Pep smirked at Aris before checking to see that the passageway was still clear of people. When he was certain he was unobserved, Pep ran his fingers across the wall in a circular motion. To Aris's astonishment, the tiles of the wall parted.

"Quickly, get in. The gateway will only stay open for a moment and the CCTV over there won't be off for long," Pep spoke with urgency. Aris hurried through as Pep followed behind.

As the two men walked down the long entrance corridor, Aris took an inquisitive look over his shoulder as the bricks sprung back to life and sealed the entrance, as the metal door re-emerged.

"How did you do that? Is it mechanics or magic?!" Aris exclaimed.

"From a certain perspective, one could call it magic. Like many things around here, it's secret, one that can only be revealed to you in time," Pep said as he guided Aris into a side room.

"Take a seat. Where have you been? To see your father? Or to see Maya?" Pep asked as he closed the door and watched Aris sit down.

"You've been spying on me for a while, haven't you?"

"And you've been spying on me." They stared sternly into each other's eyes.

"Maya," Aris replied, "I went to see Maya."

"I appreciate you want to share this experience with someone you're close to, but Maya can't be a part of this world, Aris. To share any glimpse into it is not fair on her. You understand that, right?"

"I understand that. But Maya's different. If there's anyone more worthy to becoming a Seecher, it's her. And she's good. She's amazing. I'd have no doubt that she would pass the test. She's your best research associate," Aris spoke from the heart.

"It's got nothing to do with her abilities, Aris. It's the promise I've made." Pep looked at him.

"Can't I just bring her here and you talk to her about taking the test so she can decide herself?" Aris pressed.

"No, Aris. That's exactly what I've given my word not to do! It's not up to us to bring Maya into this world. Not against the wishes of her father."

"This promise to her father, does it concern her mother?"

"Part of that promise, yes, was made when Monica died."

"You won't train Maya because her mother killed herself?" Aris had nothing else to lose.

"That's not the whole picture. Where did you hear that?"

"Maya told me. Her dad told her last night. Is it true? Did she kill herself?" Aris probed.

"She did. From Adam's perspective, anyway," Pep replied.

Aris scrunched up his eyes.

"We must leave Adam and Maya to sort out their own family affairs. It's not for us to discuss this any further until it has been resolved between those two. Agreed?" Pep intoned.

"Yes. Okay. Agreed." Pep was probably right. *Knowing Maya, once her and her father speak again about it, she'll almost certainly get her way and be here soon enough,* Aris thought.

"Today's about you. All the others have undergone the testing. Now, it's your turn."

"How did they get on?" Aris asked.

"Some have shown potential and wish to stay, whilst others have not," Pep answered.

Aris listened to the words, and his mind wondered back to his friends Leo, Thomas, and Abi.

"What? I'm the last one?"

"Yes. And it's time for you to decide. Do you want to be tested or not?" Pep asked.

Everything is so secretive. What the hell is this test, and what will it prove exactly?

"Okay, Professor, but first, I need to have some idea of what I'm doing. No one has told us what we have to do for this test. And what does it even show? How much of this stuff I have in my brain? Does it tell you I'm Seecher? And while we're on it, what does that even mean? I'm not certain I want to take a test, where the outcome means I can't share it with Maya. Look, I'm sorry, Professor, but I can't make this kind of commitment to you. Maya means far more to me than any of this. If I'm going to take your test, I need to know why I'm taking it." Aris stood up.

"Aris, it's not that I don't want to provide you with the answers. I just need you to have a clear mind to take the test and possibly go on to become a Seecher because you have a desire for greater understanding of the truth about this world and you want to be a part of helping the balance, not because you desire the powers that we yield. This is how it's done. If I share with you all the answers you say you need, I will never be sure of what compelled you to make your decision."

"Fine. Well, here is where we part ways." Aris sighed and made his way for the door.

As Aris's hand gripped the handle, Pep's voice rang out, "Wait."

Aris turned to look at Pep.

"I'll show you what I can, but on one condition."

"What?" Aris replied.

"You promise me that once I've shown you the answers, you'll not share this with Maya or anyone else. Not even the other Potentials. Can you agree to that?"

Aris took in a deep breath. "Fine. I give you my word," Aris said as Pep rose to his feet.

"Come with me."

Pep led the way to another room. He circled his hand across the door in much the same way as he did in the underground. The door opened. They entered, and Aris let out a little gasp. The room was the same as the one he'd seen in the university the day he'd followed Pep. Another mirrored room.

"What's this?" Aris asked.

"It's a mirror," Pep responded. "Now, everything I'm about to show you is real, no illusions, and as you promised me last night, you need to have an open mind."

"Okay," Aris replied, thinking back to the events of last night, his broken nose, and how they'd escaped.

Pep took out a glass Klein bottle on a neckless from under his jacket. It glowed. A bright dazzling blue light shone from it.

"This is my Key. My Seecher Key. All Seechers have one. Without it, they'd die. It is, in essence, a fragment of something that's truly pure. It's been taken out, from their dream. A Seecher Key is an extension of the Seecher themselves. It's a part of them. It's the source of their abilities and capabilities," Pep said as he moved Aris in front of the mirror.

"Abilities?" Aris whispered.

"Yes. It's the source of a Seechers' power. It's the key to many a door. Now, step aside and remember, open mind." As Pep finished speaking, he flicked the Key and from it some blue liquid flew out and hit the mirror. As it made contact, the hard surface rippled into a fluid. Aris was open-mouthed.

"As I said, this Key opens many gateways. This one will take us to a place we call the Oneiri. It's where I took you last night to escape, and it's where we're going now." Pep moved forward and signalled to Aris he was about to step through.

"The answers to your questions are on the other side. Come," Pep said as he stepped through.

Aris waited a few seconds before taking a deep breath and following Pep into the mirror.

On stepping through, he was amused to find himself back in the same room with the professor. Nothing was different.

"The Oneiri's exactly the same as the normal world," Aris remarked.

"Not at all. Seechers call the normal world the Skia. And before you ask, I'll explain why soon. First, let me introduce you to the Oneiri. Come."

Pep led them out of the mirrored room and back to the place where Pep, about half an hour before, had strangely made the tiles move and they'd stepped into the wall. Now, Aris could see an open portal before him, on one side the London Underground, and on this side the Seecher hallway.

"The entrance into the London Seecher Guild, inside the Oneiri, is always open here. There are things you need to be aware of before we leave, though. In the Oneiri, you're not seen by those in the Skia. You can see them, but they can't see you."

"What, you mean we're like...ghosts?" Aris said, looking down at himself.

"In a way, perhaps, though we're not dead."

"Cool," Aris uttered.

Pep continued, "Like a ghost, if you will, anything that has the Living Reflection is completely passable. This might seem very strange, and when you pass through the Living Reflection for the first time, it's an odd experience, but you'll get used to it."

"Wow, wow, slow down. Living what? Reflection? What? Walk through people you mean? Hang on, Pep, I'm just getting my head around walking through a mirror!" Aris laughed.

"Sorry, there's so much to share with you. I don't always put things in the correct order. Do you remember that day when you cracked the answer to the Beyond Question? You gave part of the answer."

"Yes. Five!" Aris groaned.

Pep nodded. "The second part to the answer is Reflections."

"There are Five Reflections?" Aris jumped ahead as usual by asking, "What do Seechers mean by a Reflection? So, you're telling me there are five different Reflections?" Aris asked.

"Yes. Correct. You see the real world, what we call the Skia, is not made up of the things you're taught in school. There is so much more to the Skia, more to life itself, than is ever taught conventionally. The Skia is another way to describe the physical world. But the real truth is, that the Skia is made up of, what we the Seechers call, the Five Reflections. And those Five Reflections each provide a specific structure to the Skia universe. Without the Five Reflections, there would be no Skia. The Reflections are the underlying construct of our physical reality."

Aris interrupted, "What are the Five Reflections?"

"You're eager to learn, that will serve you well. But remember, Aris, you can't study everything in a day." Pep winked at Aris before he continued, "There is Aeon, the Life Reflection. Everything that lives is made up from this Reflection. Then there is Nous, the mind Reflection. Everything that is thought or can be known is make up from this Reflection. Then there's Keno, the space Reflection. It is the canvas on which all the other Reflections take shape. It is the space between and within all things. Kairos is the time Reflection. It is the Reflection that holds and creates time. And finally, there is the matter Reflection, which is called the Hyle. Everything that has mass, anything made of matter, is the Hyle Reflection. And now you know. The Five Reflections, exist together to give form and meaning to all of our existence in the Skia." Pep smiled at Aris.

"Hang on, the world is made up of Five Reflections. And they make up everything?"

"Yes," Pep said, surprised by Aris's willingness to accept the information.

"So, Reflections are what? What exactly do they reflect? I guess the Seechers call them Reflections for a reason? What *is* reflected, what is the *source* of those reflections?" Aris asked as his mind raced with wonder.

"Impressive. Come." Pep walked forwards.

The two men left the Seechers building and entered the tube station. People walked past them. Aris moved out of their way instinctively. He stopped and waved his hands in front of a man with a Rasta hat on, who made no response. "Gosh he really can't see me, can he?!"

"Come," Pep ordered.

As they moved along the narrow platform, avoiding the commuters in the Skia became more difficult. Aris twisted and side-stepped past. Aris had been so focused on avoiding people, that he hadn't taken in his surroundings. It wasn't until he came close to a wall and an advertising poster that he became aware of the constant peculiarity of the Oneiri. Aris attempted to read the poster, but all the words were backwards. He glanced around, everything was back to front, as though he was seeing everything through the reflection of a mirror. He stood on the spot and looked around at all the things that were in reverse.

It wasn't until someone walked right through him that he shuddered and regained his thoughts. The incident didn't hurt, nor did he feel anything lasting, but it was just extremely strange. He watched as the woman who'd just walked through him stopped for a second, shook a little as if she were cold, and then continued on her way.

"First time's always the strangest."

"Why is everything in reverse?" Aris asked.

"I know. Helpful, isn't it. Let's you know that you're not in the Skia." Pep gestured to the escalator. It wasn't long before they were outside staring at the sky.

"Finally, fresh air. The air in the Oneiri always feels a bit fresher to me," Pep said, breathing in. Aris spun around, looking at everything that was so familiar yet so strange.

"You asked if the Reflections came from somewhere else, and what they reflect."

"Yes," Aris edged closer to him.

Pep waved his hands in the air and spoke a single word, "Spilio." As he did, deep clouds appeared in the sky, which spiralled upwards.

The edges of the clouds formed shapes that resembled the walls of a cave. They continued filling the sky until they stopped directly above them. It had formed a perfect circle, which instantly glowed with fabulous bright light, of all colours. Inside the colourful circle, Aris could just make out what appeared to be, a dreamlike landscape. It was like no other he'd ever seen before. Plush, peaceful, and serene, with many bright blue shining orbs of different sizes, gracefully floating in the sky.

They're the same colour as Pep's Seecher Key, Aris thought.

"All the Reflections reside from beyond there, from a place we know little about. Only a few Seechers have ventured in and returned. We call that place Nihilo. It is, as you will, a subconscious world, far beyond the walls of our reality, far greater than our own universe," Pep said as he glanced down to see Aris's face light up.

"Wow. That's…the most beautiful thing I've ever seen," Aris uttered.

"This is only a glimpse into Nihilo. A window, if you will. It is not a gateway into it," Pep finished and, as he did, he waved his hands again. The vision of Nihilo, along with the cave-like clouds in the sky, faded away.

"That's unbelievable!"

"So, you see, the Skia is made from Five Reflections that all originate from Nihilo. The Oneiri can be thought of as a looking glass through which you can see both sides of the view. In the Oneiri, you can see the Skia and Nihilo. But in the Skia, you can only see the Skia.

"A Seecher is gifted with certain abilities once they've unlocked their connection to Nihilo. This is done whilst they are in a dream state. Dreams are a powerful tool to the subconscious," Pep finished as he twiddled his Key.

"By abilities, you mean superpowers?" Aris questioned.

"Aris, in the Skia, with a Seecher Key, we're able to bend and manipulate the Reflections. It's our subconscious connection to them that effectively gives us that ability. A Seecher usually only masters one Reflection, and this can take their whole lifetime to learn," Pep said, putting his Key back.

"Is that how you fixed my nose?"

"Not quite. I fixed your nose in here. In the Oneiri. Not in the Skia."

"Oh yeah." They had already passed through the mirror when Pep took the sapphire fog to mend his nose, Aris recollected.

"This is getting very confusing," Aris said.

"Let me make it clear. In the Oneiri, Seechers cannot manipulate the Reflections like they can in the Skia because they do not respond to our commands in the Oneiri like they do in the Skia."

Aris took this in. "It's a different dimension?" Aris tried to understand.

"Exactly. There are other commands that work in the Oneiri, but not in the Skia. It's just something we learn." Aris squinted in the sunlight as Pep continued. "What we can also do here in the Oneiri is to see the energy that spreads out from Nihilo into the Skia. And it's therefore possible to carefully take some of that energy. But we must always be mindful to keep the balance."

"Energy?" Aris asked.

"This will be the last thing I show you before you decide about your testing," Pep said as he waved his hands high. "Tyche," he commanded.

Instantly, streams of light filled their surroundings. Colours of every description, of every intensity, filled the sky and stretched as far as the eye could see. They were steams of different coloured energies, moving at different speeds, all different lengths and widths. Like a time-lapse photograph of traffic on a busy road but moving all around them.

"One of the many duties we Seechers are tasked with, is to ensure the balance of the waves is kept stable in the Oneiri."

Aris's eyes were wide open. *This is possibly the most magical moment of my entire life.*

"Wow, you see that!" Pep shrieked. "That black wave over there?" Pep pointed, and Aris saw a thick black energy engulfing a person walking out of a bank.

"That's a lot of negative energy he's got following him." Pep smiled. Aris's mind was blown.

"What does that mean for him?" Aris asked.

"It will, no doubt, surround him until he encounters a rather unpleasant experience. Negative energy's stubborn to shake off once it's got hold of you like that." Pep chuckled quietly.

Aris wondered, "Like what?"

Pep replied, "He might lose all his money, become bankrupt. His life will start to spiral out of control. Maybe start drinking, who knows how it will affect him. End up in a car crash."

"Shit," Aris said, but Pep moved on.

"Well, well, well. That's a sight." Pep pointed.

"What?" Aris tried to see, too. "Look over there. You see that jade green? That's fortune. Something very good is going to happen to her. And that red, it's passion. Oh la-la. And over there, you see that blue, that magnificent sapphire blue?!"

Aris did see it and also recognized it. "That's what you healed my nose with!" he said triumphantly.

"Yes, that's health."

"You picked it up in your hands."

"Yes. Seechers can move the energy waves around in the Oneiri. It's not that hard. But we can never create energy ourselves, nor can we destroy it. But we can move it."

As Pep said this, he took his arm back and thrust it forwards shouting, "Kinesis," towards the man with the black energy around him. Aris gasped as the black energy went flying off the man and up into the sky. Pep turned to Aris.

"See, it just keeps moving around. The Seecher Covenant demands we keep the equilibrium balanced for the sake of the Skia. That the waves are never made unbalanced. Little changes like fixing your nose are things we, at times, are permitted to do. Although, be warned, even the simplest of changes to the energy field can cause dramatic and sometimes catastrophic consequences. That's why we maintain a balance and don't manipulate the waves to suit our own selfish needs," Pep said, looking at his watch.

"Oh my, time has escaped us. We must be gone,"

"This is unbelievable!" Aris whispered as Pep waved his hands.

"No Tyche." The energy field was no longer visible.

"Bloody hell. So here in the Oneiri, you keep the balance of the energies that come from Nihilo, and in the Skia, you can manipulate the Five Reflections. But for what? You said you're tasked with more than just the balance. What are you tasked with?"

"In the Skia, Seechers must protect this ancient knowledge at all costs. This knowledge, this power, in the wrong hands, is unthinkably dangerous. That's why there's a code we keep and, fundamentally, that code instructs us to protect Nihilo and all its secrets. And that's exactly what the Seechers have done for nearly three thousand years."

"I want to be a Seecher," Aris declared.

"Aris. I said I think you might be a Potential. As in, you have a connection to Nihilo we could possibly unlock, but only if you have enough Epsilon in your pineal gland to do so. This is the energy that connects us directly to Nihilo. We can unlock that Epsilon in a dream and place it into something like this," Pep held up his Key. "This then can be used by a Seecher to interact with our world, and beyond."

"So, the test is to see if I have enough Epsilon in my brain that can be taken out and made into a Seecher Key?" Aris asked as they walked through the underground station.

"Precisely." Pep grinned. "Let us go and find out."

Adam wondered how long he'd been trapped inside the room. He'd attempted on a few occasions to reveal the Tyche, but there was no energy he could use. There were only negative waves, probably echoing his misfortune. *It must be nearly twelve hours I've been here,* he thought. He again tried to open the door, straining hard to operate the handle. It wouldn't move. It was still locked and, therefore, there was no way of him opening it whilst still in the Oneiri.

Glaring at his reflection in the mirror, he took out his Seecher Key and wondered what the best course of action to take was.

"Tallia will take you through the testing," Pep said as he walked Aris into Tallia's office.

She sat at her desk, finishing off paperwork from the other Potential's results. The room was filled with all manner of strange plants. Tropical vegetation filled shelf after shelf. An entire cabinet contained exotic flowers, which each required unique conditions to survive, conditions that this dimly lit, dry-aired room must fail to offer them. But still, the flora defiantly thrived. He noticed a few small animals milling quietly around the room, hiding in the cracks and shadows, like voles and hedgehogs. A baby fox slept in a dog bed.

"Hi, Aris. Quiet not to disturb the animals," she whispered. "Are you here to take the test?"

"Yes."

Pep leant down and stroked the baby fox before leaving.

Tallia directed Aris to sit in the empty chair.

"Right. Well, the test is painless, and you'll be asleep for most of it. All you need do is to lie on a special table, we call the Mirror Sands. Once on it, you'll close your eyes and relax. There'll be a slightly strange sensation before you drift off to sleep. When you awake, we'll have the answer as to whether you have the potential to become a Seecher or not."

"So, the point of it is to find out if I've got enough Epsilon in my brain to become a Seecher. But how does it actually test for that?" Aris asked as the baby fox woke up and jumped onto Aris's lap, "Aww, hello little fella."

"His name's Pixel."

Aris stroked the little fox on his lap as he listened to Tallia.

"The test scans your brain. What we're looking for is this." Tallia lifted a beautifully intricate necklace from beneath her blouse. As it came into view, it glowed a beautiful blue, which seized Aris's gaze. He could have sworn the animals, and even the plants in the room, seemed to gravitate towards it.

"The blue liquid inside this Klein bottle is Epsilon. It's a form of pure energy, directly created from Nihilo. It's the only thing in this world that's not constructed out of the Five Reflections."

For a moment, a colourful humming bird flew out of an exotic plant and danced around Tallia and the blue light before going back to the plant.

"You see, Aris, the Epsilon within this is ever-replenishing when used correctly. It's the source of our connection. This energy resides dormant in all people, but those who could be Seechers have much greater quantities of it. Epsilon has a direct effect on the Reflections around it, so to ensure it doesn't react with the Reflections it comes into contact with, it needs to be reflected in on itself. This naturally occurs within the pineal gland. Many years ago, Seechers discovered they could mimic that unique ability in these, which we now affectionately call our Seecher Keys." As Tallia finished, she placed the Key back under her blouse.

"Wow, that's amazing. So, if I have enough Epsilon, I can make a

Key like that and do the things you and Pep can do?"

"That's what the test is for. To see if there's enough for you to face the Seecher trials, and then the activation. Time's getting late, we need to start the test."

"Yeah, sorry, of course."

Tallia clapped her hands twice, and the animals who'd come out of their hiding places, scuttled back. Pixel jumped off Aris's lap and went obediently to his bed.

"Wow." Aris smiled.

Tallia gestured for Aris to leave the room with her. They walked down a corridor and into another room.

In the centre was a large table which had intricate designs all over it. The same patterns and symbols were echoed throughout the rest of the room. On the ceiling, directly above the table was a pentagram, which had five different symbols at each point and a fish in the middle. Aris stared up at it as he walked in.

"What's that?" Aris said as he pointed up.

"Those symbols represent the Five Reflections. Hyle, Keno, Aeon, Nous, and Kairos, the centre symbol represents the ability to master all the Reflections. Seechers who master all Five Reflections are called Lucasian Seechers." Tallia stood at Aris's side, pausing for a moment before continuing, "Please, lie down on the table."

Aris followed her instructions. It was soft, as though sitting on powder.

"It'll feel odd when it starts, like you're sinking into sand, but just relax, and you'll drift off into a deep sleep."

"What if I don't sleep?"

"Oh, you will," Tallia laughed, as she left the room.

Suddenly, Aris was alone in this ancient-looking room and an eerie silence consumed him. Just as he began to have doubts, a strong tingling sensation rippled down his back, and then all along the back of his legs. Tiny bits of shiny sand rose up, and then floated around his limbs. His stomach dropped, like he was sinking, but then as the tiny flecks of reflective sand rolled over his face, he fell into a deep sleep.

Tallia reached the observation room. Pep stood there, looking out at

Aris. Sel and Kat were also by his side. The four watched as the mirror sands floated around Aris, and then drifted into the air. Tiny grains of reflection sparkled in the light. They twirled in the air above Aris until they created a prefect 3D replica of his brain. Aris remained fast asleep, dreaming.

"That was quick! The mirror sands usually take much longer to reflect the participants brain. Let me just change the vibrations to view the amount of Epsilon," Tallia said as she moved some dials on the wall just below the observation area.

The mirror particles changed colour, and parts of the brain seemed to become grey and indistinguishable from one another. Then the pineal gland appeared, a small faint blue glow sliding into view.

"That can't be right," Pep whispered.

Tallia fiddled with more dials, and the brain became clearer, but the blue colour of the pineal gland remained faint.

"That doesn't look Potential to me, Pep. Surely that's less Epsilon than you'd get in an average person," Sel said in a deep voice.

Kat and Sel turned for the door. To them the question had been answered, but Pep's eyes caught a glimmer of something strange.

"Did you see that, Tallia? The Epsilon pulsated," Pep said.

"No," Tallia quizzed.

"Epsilon cannot exist in the body, other than in the pineal gland," Sel said as he turned back to watch.

"Can you change the harmonics to give a full body scan?" Pep asked.

"I can, but why?" Tallia asked.

Tallia followed the order anyway. The mirror sands rippled out and re-formed into a full-scale replica of Aris's body. Tallia touched a few more dials and within an instant all four were struck by an unbelievable sight. The room burst into deep blue light.

"Not possible," Kat whispered, her voice a faint whisper.

"How?" Tallia said, as she quickly turned a few more dials.

The colour dimmed as she changed the frequencies that controlled the mirror sands. The four were completely stunned as they witnessed blue Epsilon light pumping through the replica body, following what appeared to be the veins and arteries.

"It looks like the Epsilon's being pumped around his entire body! Through his blood," Sel remarked.

"That amount of Epsilon is far more than I've ever seen in my life," Pep confessed.

"How is it remaining stable in his blood?" Kat wondered. "I would have thought that would be impossible."

"I don't have any answers right now. I have no choice but to consult the other Elders. But have no doubt about it, there is clearly something extraordinarily special about Aris Fletcher," Pep spoke as he peered through the observation window, his eyes falling onto the dreaming young man.

"Has any Seecher ever had this much Epsilon?" Kat asked.

"Lucasians," Sel whispered as he turned to Pep, who still stared into the chamber.

Pep nodded as he heard Sel's faint reply.

"Lucasians would definitely have greater amounts of Epsilon, but I've never met one, nor have I heard that they have Epsilon in their blood," Pep uttered as his gaze moved up from Aris and on to the reflective mirror sand body just above as bright blue shining light circulated through the entire image.

It had been over twenty-four hours. Adam stared in anguish at the door. The small room he found himself trapped inside, grew smaller by the hour. He'd waited for someone to come in, strained to hear conversations in the corridor. But he'd not seen nor heard anything. He was no further on from understanding who had set this trap than when he'd first walked in. He was also no closer to escaping. Did anyone even know he was missing?

No doubt, the Seechers will think I'm still with Maya, and Maya will probably assume I've left early to go on my trip. I'm on my own, he thought.

There was no one else he could think of who'd realize he was missing, let alone have any idea what kind of mess he was in.

"Another day of waiting in here and I'll be in no state to do anything," he spoke as he reached for his Key. *I need to try soon. Make my move or I'll die in here.* He held onto that thought before making a decision. It was time. Time for those who had locked him in to experience what a Seecher can really do.

He aimed his Key and flicked some blue light onto his hand. He quickly rubbed the light in between both hands, and the air around them seemed to distort. "Ready!"

Moving to the mirror directly in front of the door, he flicked more light from his Key onto the mirror. It rippled like a river, and Adam quickly jumped through.

Leaving the Oneiri and entering the Skia, Adam flung his hands towards the door. The wood instantly decayed. The steel fittings rusted and aged at a rapid speed before his very eyes and, soon, the door had aged some eight hundred years and fell away.

Dr Rivers watched on the CCTV camera in complete amazement as the tall broad man stepped from the mirror and into the room. He had read about the Seechers moving in and out of reflections, but seeing it for real, with his own eyes, was astounding. He could see the door on another screen. He watched as the door fell apart within a matter of seconds.

"Truly amazing. What power they possess. Power of the gods," Dr Rivers spoke towards the screen. He turned to the security agent sat to his left side.

"Activate the floor," Dr Rivers demanded.

The man flicked a switch.

Adam watched as the door came away from the eroded hinges and decayed into charcoal. He could see through the door frame that the corridor was clear, but before he could edge out of the room, a high-pitched *click* reverberated.

Whilst his focus had been fixed on aging the door and his escape, he'd been completely oblivious to the change in the floor. Lots of small metallic circles appeared dotted across the ground, as if from nowhere. Before Adam could take a step towards freedom, the room was filled with bright yellow flashes and the deafening sound of crackling electricity.

Thick yellow bolts of electricity arched up high from the metallic spots on the floor and appeared to tangle and puncture Adam's body. He attempted to grab his Key, intending to bend a Reflection, but it was too late.

Muscles throughout his entire body went into spasm. It was suddenly impossible to grab his Key or use the remaining Epsilon on his hands. Within seconds, both his legs had become stiff. He lost his balance, then crashed to the floor. Adam jolted and flipped on the ground. Yellow bolts stabbed at his body. His mind clouded over and blood seeped from a wound on his head. His hands twitched in spasm at his sides.

As he became motionless, the volts of mysterious yellow lightening stopped. Adam now rested on the floor, unconscious. Still. His Seecher Key dangling out of his shirt, in full view.

REFLECTIONS REVEALED

Maya woke early. She turned to her side, grabbed her phone off charge, and scrolled through her messages. She'd hoped to see one from her dad, but there was still nothing. She'd not heard anything from him for nearly two days, and all her messages had been delivered but not read. She was concerned she'd hurt him far more than she'd intended. Perhaps this was why he hadn't even read her messages. It wasn't uncommon for him to leave spontaneously for work without saying goodbye to her. However, he would usually have made some sort of effort to message her and keep her updated.

She typed another message to apologize for their argument and to let him know she loved him dearly, and that they should talk tonight.

Going through her morning routine, Maya soon found herself at the university library. She needed to cram in some much-needed study. She had an important exam on Friday. She read over some journals spread over her library desk. The content was heavy. Trying to focus on the subject of meta-emotion, the topic of the forthcoming exam, was almost impossible. After ten minutes of reading, she was back to her phone, ringing Aris.

He didn't answer. The phone went to voicemail, and Maya was quick to write him a text message, which would be the third she'd sent him without reply.

Adam's consciousness slowly returned. A sharp splitting pain stemmed from the right side of his head. Large areas of his body had been badly burnt, by the yellow currents. He awoke in a dimly lit room, tied to a chair by both his feet and hands. He couldn't move a single muscle.

"I was concerned for a moment we might've killed you," Dr Rivers said as his thin pale face came into view. "We've never tested that system on a person before."

Adam squinted his eyes but remained silent.

"If I were you, I'd be wondering who I am? And, of course, how on earth I've managed to capture a Seecher?" Dr Rivers said, coming closer to Adam. "All valid questions. Except, the problem is, I'm only here to ask you questions, not answer any." Dr Rivers towered over him.

"I'm not... Answering... Anything." Adam found it hard to reply as the concussion and injuries impeded his senses.

"You will." Dr Rivers pulled out a chair from the corner and perched in front of him. "You see, if you fail to give me adequate answers, we'll simply extract the information directly from your mind, probing your memories until we have what we need. We know a lot about you Seechers, and about the source of your power. Ripping your mind apart to get the answers I need is well within my capabilities. It's not something I *want* to do, but if you make this too difficult, you'll be wishing that we had killed you." Dr Rivers meant every word. He held no regard for those he'd trampled on to get to where he was today. Destroying the Seecher in front of him, to acquire knowledge, was well within his corrupt moral code. A justifiable fatality.

Adam was too weak to reply.

Dr Rivers folded his arms as he spoke. "My issue with the Seechers is that you're monopolising the greatest power that this world's ever known. And yet, no one's trying to stop you. Because no one knows you exist! Apart from us, that is." Dr Rivers beamed.

"How many of you wretched gatekeepers are there? Five thousand? Perhaps more? Soon, I'll have the means to seek and destroy every Seecher on this planet. And then, the source of your power, Nihilo..." Dr Rivers paused as panic cross Adam's face at the mention of the subconscious world. "Oh, we know all about the origins of your power, the Great Mystery you hoard and conceal from the world. Your selfish ways will soon be exposed and the domination of the Seechers will come to its fateful end. And I will bring this power to the people. To heal the sick, to end starvation, to make a better world. All of that will have started here. With this." Dr Rivers removed a small box from his jacket. He opened it to display Adam's glowing Seecher Key. "This truly wondrous substance here."

Adam's expression cracked as terror seeped across his face.

"You know, we've spent what feels like a lifetime, perfecting our extraction technique, yet we only ever seem to be able to produce a dull yellow form of Epsilac. But when you Seechers extract it, it's this glorious blue Epsilon. Totally pure. Perfect, I hear. I want to know how you achieve this. What do you do that keeps it in its original form? What is it we're not doing? I'll be back soon. You can prepare your answer whilst you wait." Dr Rivers slapped his thighs as he stood up and left.

Adam watched the silhouette of his captor, stood on the other side of the glass door.

"Simon, prepare our guest for the subconscious probe. Don't extract any data yet. I don't want his mind damaged. Just map out the Epsilon signature for the new drive. We'll use this to power it. This is the missing piece to our puzzle." Dr Rivers held up the glowing blue Seecher Key like a prize trophy.

"The technicians are ready. They say as soon as they have the readout, they can print a new drive. And you want to power it, with that?" Simon pointed at the Seecher Key.

"Absolutely. I'm not taking any chances this time. Our failures in the past have been, in part, down to the data not being accurate enough. But what's truly to blame for our failure is the impurity of the power source itself. Now, with this, we'll be able to identify and locate every Seecher and Potential Seecher on the entire planet." Dr Rivers put the Key back into the box. "Call everyone back in. We need everyone working." As he finished, Dr Rivers turned to Dr Pine, who'd joined the discussion and sheepishly stood behind Simon. "Take this and guard it with your life." Dr Rivers handed the box to him.

"Yes, sir, of course, I shall. However, I don't wish to alarm you, but the old texts I've studied make it very clear how fatal it is for a Seecher to be without their Key for too long. Also, it would probably be wise if we let medical treat his wounds and monitor his health. We don't want him getting an infection before the data extraction. It could corrupt the information," Dr Pine said, in the hope that his boss might show some humanity.

"He needs no treatment! The Seecher will survive a day or two longer. We'll use the drive before he perishes," Dr Pine bravely interrupted him. "But, sir…"

Dr Rivers rolled his eyes. "Fine, you can make sure we keep the Key in close enough proximity to him to ensure he doesn't die before we have everything we need. Now go! Get ready!" Dr Rivers ushered them away with a flick of his hand.

Dr Pine headed off with the box. Simon came in closer to Dr Rivers. "What about the directors? Have you informed them yet?"

"No. I don't intend to inform them right this minute. I'll let them know as soon as I have the completed hard drive. Then they can truly understand my worth," As Dr Rivers finished, he glanced through the glass at Adam and rubbed his hands together gleefully.

The beginning of the dream played out the same as it had so many times before. Aris was on the roof of a building. Maya stood in front of him, demanding he hand over the blue shining glass in his hands. He refuses and, soon after, a gun goes off. A deep surge rips through Aris, and he sees himself fall from the building and into the river below.

But as he collided with the water, the dream suddenly took a different turn. He now stood drenched in Maya's dining room. In front of him, Adam sat tied to a chair. His skin a patchwork of raw, burnt tissue. Blood matted his hair and trickled down the right-hand side of his face, from a nasty gaping head wound. Aris tentatively walked towards him. As he got closer, Adam shouted at Aris, "You can save me! You can save us all!" With that, Aris awoke.

It took him a few minutes to remember where he was. The last day had been such a whirlwind. For a second, he wondered if everything Pep had showed him, and what Tallia had told him, was all just another dream. He wondered what the last thing he could remember was. It didn't take him long to recall the events that led to him lying down on the testing table. He remembered the strange sensation of the mirror sands and falling into a deep sleep.

"How long have I been asleep for?" he said aloud, realising he wasn't alone and was back in the in the Seecher building's dorm.

"About eighteen hours," came the reply. "Potentials usually have a very prolonged and deep sleep following the testing," Tallia continued as she stepped into view.

"What? That's ridiculous!"

"We try not to wake anyone following the testing, just let them sleep it out. Dreams can reveal a lot about ourselves and our journeys ahead." Tallia offered him a glass of water. "Drink a lot today. You need to rehydrate."

Aris took the glass and knocked back the water. He was so thirsty.

"Is the test complete then? Do I have enough Epsilon? Can I become a Seecher?" Aris fired off. Tallia took the empty glass from him and placed it on a desk.

"We did complete the test, and…" Aris hung on her every word.

"And?"

"Congratulations, if you choose to, you can indeed become a Seecher."

"Really? Without sounding arrogant, I kind of knew it. If that makes sense," Aris replied with a huge smile across his face.

"Seechers know they're destined for much bigger things," Tallia replied.

"Where's Pep?" Aris asked.

"He had to go and see the other Guild Elders. There are many Seechers, set up in different guilds around the world. Each one has a Pep of their own. He's gone to discuss a few things with the other Elders," Tallia said as she handed Aris some clean clothes. "We had to move you whilst you were asleep, but we didn't change you, so you've been in those clothes for nearly two days now. Might be good to have a shower and a change. You should freshen up before you come and meet the rest, who have positive test results."

Tallia continued to tell Aris about his close friends. Thomas and Abi waited downstairs with the four others who've been identified as Potential Seechers. Sadly, Leo was not one of them. Tallia explained to Aris that Leo didn't have enough Epsilon, and that Kat had used her mind Reflection skills to manipulate and erase Leo's memories of the last few days. Everything about the Seechers had been removed from his mind.

After he took a shower and got changed, Aris called his dad to check that he was okay. Peter was now out of hospital and back home. Aris explained he was staying at a friend's house for a few days to get his revision done. Aris was happy to hear his dad had some support from a home-help company arranged by the hospital, and that Mrs Potter, was over at the moment, cooking for him. Hearing his dad's grumpy old voice again, knowing he was okay and getting help, was a big relief.

Aris headed off to meet Thomas and Abi. They talked for a few hours sharing their experiences of the testing. Exchanging what they knew so far, about the Seechers. They tried to anticipate what lay ahead of them, why Maya wasn't there, and that remaining here for the time being was their safest option. In the excitement, Aris's dream had been forgotten.

Dr Rivers watched as Adam lay unconscious on an examination table. Adam's face and head had sensors affixed at various points. These were wired up to other scientific instruments. A large screen behind him had jumbled Greek numbers and letters, flashing on and off. The system stabilised. Several technicians moved around the table. Others adjusted different parameters on several of the computers dotted around the lab. As the system continued, the characters on the screen constructed a more coherent pattern until a sequence of letters and numbers were clear and fixed.

"That's it. That's the frequency setting for the waves," Dr Rivers said as the technicians in the room burst into applause.

"We need to get this algorithm to all the analysts. We're going to need everyone to work on the translation software. We want to work out how to translate this into geographical data once we activate the hard drive. How long until the new hard drive can be constructed from this data?" Dr Rivers spoke to Dr Pine, who was at his side, sharing in the jubilation.

"The glass printers will work on it straight away, but it's a slow process. It'll take two days. If we're lucky, one day. But really, it needs two," Dr Pine replied.

"Get it done fast as you can, but don't cut any corners. I want this drive to be flawless," Dr Rivers replied as he stepped closer to the screen, his hands rubbing swiftly together.

***

Maya walked into the office and made her way to her desk. She'd been called into Curative Analytical on urgent instruction, which threatened that if she didn't come in, her internship would be cancelled. As she walked in, she was shocked to see how busy it was. The whole building had erupted with activity. She'd never seen this many members of staff here, ever. She asked a few other analysts what was happening, but no one could give her a clear explanation. The only thing she could gauge was that they had a new source of data, and it was producing more information in a day than the system had processed in over a year. So much information that they required everyone in, to work on it.

Maya sat at her desk and turned on her computer as Simon came over to give her some orders.

"Maya, well done for coming in. You'll be given a packet of information. Dr Rivers wants you to work on producing an algorithm based on the information generated from a specific cypher."

"Do you mean the same as before? Will I get to review any of the output information?" Maya asked.

"No, just the original information. We need you to work on ways of decrypting it," Simon said dismissively.

"Okay, but you do appreciate that without knowing or reviewing the output data, makes what you're asking me to do pretty much impossible," Maya replied, not sure if Simon grasped the actual intricacies of his request.

"Well, you better start now then, and less of the back chat. It's not an attractive quality for a young lady to have," Simon snapped back.

Maya snarled at his tone. She wondered what she was doing there and not in the library revising for her exam. However, this internship had gotten her this far, and she couldn't risk losing it today. She spent a few hours trying to work on producing what was being asked, but every time she completed something, she had no way of determining if it worked, as she couldn't run it on any data.

She tried using the algorithms she had worked on before. Some of it produced similar results to what she had demonstrated in the past, others didn't. But since she didn't really know what she was testing, she was unsure if any of the algorithms she had produced were correct. All she could do was rank them in order of what she thought *would* work.

Throughout the day, Maya looked around the extremely busy office. She was a little taken aback by just how many security officers walked round. Most had guns. She'd never seen armed private security guards there before.

It was nearing the end of the day, and Maya was close to stopping and heading home when Simon returned. She noticed he, too, carried a weapon. She watched as he walked to his desk and placed the gun into his top draw and locked it. She looked away and pretended to busy herself as he made his way over to her.

"How are you coming along? Dr Rivers has high hopes you're going to show us all up again," Simon told her.

"I've got about six programs that could work. But we won't know until we start trying them. When will we get the data?" she replied.

"Two days, I'm told. Two days, and we'll have as much data as you need," Simon replied.

Maya watched as he headed off. Once he was out of sight, she packed up her stuff and left the office.

Aris's day had been filled with discussion with the other Potentials. They had even begun to read some ancient Seecher texts. Meeting and chatting with the other Potentials had been exciting. Aris knew Abi and Thomas, but he also made new friends in Aaron, Jemma, Sam and Max. The texts, on the other hand, were a little dull and slow going.

The seven Potentials had all been given books on the Seecher Covenant. Hoping to learn more about the Great Mystery, Aris was a little disappointed they were mainly to do with the Seechers' code of conduct. The Covenants were largely the work of three ancient Lucasian Seechers, who each, at different times, had accessed Nihilo and returned.

It was late in the evening, and most of the Potentials had retired to their designated sleeping quarters. It was only, Aris and Thomas still up discussing the Seechers, when Pep walked in.

"Good evening, gentlemen," Pep whispered, trying not to startle them.

The two men jumped to their feet.

"Pep," Aris uttered.

"Do you mind if I interrupt you to have a quiet word with Aris?"

Thomas shuffled on the spot, gesturing good night as he quickly left the room. Pep closed the door and made his way to one of the chairs.

"How has your first day as a Seecher Potential been?" Pep asked.

"Amazing."

"Good."

"How's your day been?" Aris mumbled.

"I had to convene an urgent meeting. Something occurred yesterday which hasn't ever happened to me before," Pep replied.

"Really? What was it?" Aris asked.

"You, Aris," Pep said in a soft tone.

"Me?"

"Yes. I promised I wouldn't lie to you. To honour that, and for you to carry on this journey, I need to tell you something very peculiar occurred during your testing," Pep remained calm.

"What? I'm still a Potential, right?"

"Yes, you're still a Potential. As you know, we measure a person's potential by the presence and amount of Epsilon they have. You have a great deal more than I've ever seen in anyone before. There's just one thing that's very different," Pep continued.

"What? What is it?"

"The Epsilon within you isn't in the area of your brain where it should be. It's running throughout your entire body. Pumping around you, through your blood."

"What does that mean? I can still become a Seecher and make a Key right?"

"If I'm honest, I don't have the answers to those questions, right now. We're currently unsure if the activation process will work for you. But we're confident you have the Potential to be a Seecher. In fact, a few Elders seem to think this has happened in the past. Just not in recent memory. The other Seecher Elders are, as we speak, searching ancient texts to try and shed more light on the situation. We won't do anything that puts you at risk, hence why we're looking into it first. Does that make sense?"

"Yes, I guess."

"Great. It's important you're aware of the situation. I was worried that, with everything else, it might be too much. You have proven my faith to be well-placed." Pep put a firm hand on Aris's shoulder before standing up.

Pep left Aris to rest, with clear instructions to stay in the guild for the time being and not to leave. Aris gave him a half-nod in agreement. Though, once all the lights were off, Aris snuck out.

Maya let Aris in. She was as delighted to see him, as he was her. They soon found themselves having their third kiss. They'd not seen each other for three days now.

"Have you been okay? Things are crazy. Really, really crazy," Aris declared as he strode into her dining room. When he arrived, he looked at the table, and the memory of his dream of Adam flashed back into his mind, for the first time since he had it. He turned to ask Maya, "Where's your dad?"

"He's not back yet. I've not heard from him since he left." Maya frowned.

"He hasn't been at the Seechers Headquarters, either. Where do you think, he is?"

Maya wasn't sure. "I just don't know."

Aris shared Maya's unease. "I had a dream about him. He was right here, in a lot of pain, strapped to a chair. He shouted at me to save him."

"Have you told the Seechers about this?"

"No, I just remembered it now. So much has been going on," Aris replied, feeling a little stupid.

Maya was angry he hadn't mentioned it to anyone until now. Aris attempted to calm her. "Maya, seriously it might be nothing. It wasn't until I walked in here that it came flooding back…and gave me that feeling."

"What feeling?" Maya demanded.

Aris gulped, "The same feeling I got when I had the other dreams about the kidnapping, and the times when I knew my dad was unwell."

"Aris, I haven't heard from him for days now. I thought it was okay, but it's been too long. It's not normal. If he isn't with the Seechers then where is he? Surely, he should be with them?! Where else would he be?"

"I'll ask Pep as soon as I get back. He'll know. He's probably away on some business. Pep has left a few times. I'm sorry. I've just been bogged down with the test. I slept for like eighteen hours after it. And since then, they've made me read a text called the Seecher Covenant. I'll have to agree to abide by it before I can take the Seecher trials, and then the activation," Aris explained.

"Covenant, trials, activation?!" Maya exclaimed. "So, they're going to train you then?"

"Yes. I can't go into too much detail right now, but everything you thought you know about them, times that by like a million and that's just how weird and wonderful it really is. It's so much more than anything we could have imagined. Once I'm a Seecher, I'll train you myself."

Maya smiled at Aris's commitment to her. Maybe one day, she too, will have access to the secrets of the Seechers, even without her dad's permission. But she couldn't help but worry about him now.

"Thomas and Abi are Potentials, as well," Aris said without thinking.

"Great. You're in, and so are my two best friends, and here I am studying for Friday's exam! How stupid am I? Did I mention that I almost lost my internship, as well. Why is my world falling apart? Shit, Aris, I've not heard from dad since I told him I wished he was dead, three fucking days ago! Now your dream! I'm seriously worried. I think I should call the police," Maya said, picking up her phone.

"I'll go back now and tell the Seechers your dad is missing and tell them about my dream of him being captured. If something's wrong, they'll have more chance of finding him than the police, I bet. I'll call you from there," Aris said as he moved close and placed a consoling arm around her shoulders.

———

When Aris returned to the London Guild, he managed to find Kat, who was still up. He told her about his dream and Maya's concerns about Adam. Kat went and woke Sel, and the two Seechers took Aris's alarm very seriously, promising to do all they could to find out what had happened to Adam.

"He's not on any known business. But that doesn't mean he isn't. Sometimes, we can be given missions by the Elders in secret. Pep will know for sure," Sel said as he walked Aris to a small room just away from the Mirror Sands. Kat followed closely.

"I'll get Tallia to speak with Maya in the morning," Kat said as the three entered the room and closed the door behind them.

"What's this?" Aris asked looking at the bizarre chair in front of him. It was a glass chair, which had a large glass ball, about a meter wide, floating directly above it, with five smaller glass balls orbiting around the larger one.

"It's called *Plato's Oculus*. It allows Seechers to project their dreams and memories, like a film. We can then record it. You probably know by now that dreams are extremely important to the Seechers. They are often the first insight from Nihilo," Kat said as she directed Aris to the chair.

"Don't worry, Aris. It's painless and harmless. All you need to do is focus on the memory of the dream," Sel said as he moved to a control panel.

As Aris sat down on the chair, Kat rotated the glass helmet over onto his head. The helmet was attached to the larger glass ball that now spun above his head.

"Remember, just focus on the dream," Sel insisted. "Are you ready?"

"Sure," Aris replied.

Sel flicked a switch, and the small glass balls sped up, moving rapidly around the larger ball as a glowing blue light flickered in the centre. Moments later, images appeared within the large ball. It was Aris's dream of Adam being tied to the chair. It wasn't crisp and clear, but both Kat and Sel could make out enough of the image to fill them with concern.

"That's enough. I think we have most of the dream there," Sel said as he pressed a few more buttons to transfer the images to the memory of the machine.

"That's it? That was quick," Aris said as Kat removed the helmet.

"Yeah, you were good at the recall. The dream was right there," Kat replied.

"So, what do you think? Is he alright?" Aris asked.

"We saw what you saw. It's natural to be concerned by a dream like that. We'll look into it now, but don't worry too much. Some dreams are just dreams," Sel said.

"Are you going to check with Pep if Adam's on a mission?" Aris pried further.

"Yes. We'll ask him first thing. But I wouldn't be too alarmed, Aris," Kat said. "Now, go get some sleep. We'll follow up with you in the morning."

Aris left the room and called Maya to tell her they would know for sure if Adam is really on a secret Seecher mission in the morning, but they now knew about his dream of Adam and her concerns.

Maya felt a deep sense of relief. Finally, she would have some answers as to her father's whereabouts. She would sleep better knowing this.

As soon as Kat and Sel were alone, they shared a look of deep concern. They both knew something wasn't right, and it couldn't wait. Moments later, they woke up Pep and Tallia and explained about Adam's disappearance and Aris's dream.

Maya entered the Curative Analytical building very early. She was surprised to see the place was still super busy. As she made her way to her desk, she saw a couple of analysts were already working away. She walked by a few more women at the coffee machine, waiting to get their fix. Maya overheard a snippet of their conversation.

"Well, apparently, it's a person they have."

"No?! Surely not," another woman gasped.

The gossiper continued, and Maya strained to hear more.

"Yes. Seriously, there's an actual person up there on the security level. He's apparently giving them the data we're going to be analysing. Well, that's what Martin in security told Helen in accounting."

Maya finally reached her desk. She brought up the programs she worked on. She tried to focus, but something niggled away at her, something about the last two days in the office that deeply unsettled her.

She took out a flash drive from her pocket and connected it to the computer. She had to work around the systems software that stopped external devices from being attached, but that was easy for her. She had hacked parts of the system already, and the flash drive had some of her viruses and malware she'd used in the past.

Maya launched a few programs through her USB stick and broke down the system's firewalls and protections. She wasn't sure what she was looking for.

She stumbled across a few files: Epsilac Project, Tauredunum Raiders, Professor Mielikki's work, The Omega Project. There were lots of different systems all connected to the main server. She ignored it all. She continued scanning the system for anything linked to what she'd overheard. Taking extra precautions to cover her tracks, it was then she saw something that chilled her to the core: *Seecher Tracking Initiative.*

She quickly gained access to that server. It took her a little longer than her initial hacks but she was soon in and searching through different drives on that server. She looked over something that made her stomach flip. It was the original cypher she had produced, and the data she extrapolated regarding locations. What if the data she had been working on was related to the Seechers and Seechers' locations?

She continued searching without finding anything significant until she found a program titled CCTV of Security Level, and a file called The Hard Drive – human interface.

She hovered over the file for the hard drive for a moment, wanting to know more about what it could be and what the organization was involved in, but she didn't open it. Instead she clicked on the CCTV icon and a grid of live video streams filled her monitor. Her eyes were suddenly drawn to one corner. Her body shook involuntarily.

"Dad?!"

Aris sat in the kitchen of the Seechers headquarters with Thomas and Abi, waiting to hear from the Seechers about Adam. The three of them were taking their minds off it, by reading over books related to dreaming, according to the Seechers. Abi read aloud out of her book to the others, "Prophetic dreams are usually experienced by Nous Seechers and can be taken as glimpses into the future or reflect occurrences that have happened or are happening."

There was a large fruit bowl in the centre of the glass table. Cups, glasses, and cereal bowls littered the tabletop. The kitchen itself was quite curious, with an assortment of large plants, ancient Seecher artefacts and carvings, and some unusual objects placed around the room. When Aris's phone rang, he answered it almost immediately. It was Maya.

Maya didn't wait for him to speak.

"Dad's being held hostage at Curative Analytical!"

That was all he needed to hear before abruptly racing out of the room and sprinting to Pep's office.

Within the hour, Maya sat with Aris in Pep's office, along with Kat, Tallia, and Sel. In the centre of the room, was one of the small glass balls from the Plato's Oculus. Within it, a faint projection looped of Adam strapped to a chair, just as Aris had seen in his dream.

"That's exactly as I saw him in the CCTV footage!" Maya gasped.

"And you're sure it was him?" Kat asked, sounding as shocked as she felt.

"YES! For the third fucking time. They have my dad. They know all about Seechers. How much more proof do you need?!"

Aris had a theory he wanted to put forward. "I think they've been finding the Potentials through the testing they've been doing. Stephen Monroe took a test at Curative Analytical for money, and he went missing, and I took the test, to pay off my father's debts, and the next day, they came after me," Maya gasped.

"How did you know about this?" Kat asked.

"They were handing out flyers at University. It…" Aris didn't know how to carry on. He had no idea that taking that test would lead to being attacked.

"Well done, Aris, That's very helpful." Pep wrote this down.

"So why, or more to the point, *how* have they now got Adam?" Sel asked, thinking tactically.

Maya rolled her eyes and blurted, "We had a big argument, and I stormed off. He might well have been looking for me, that's where I have my internship."

"So, he may have gone there for other reasons, not knowing they were the new threat?" Pep thought aloud.

"Do you see that?" Tallia pointed to Adam's open shirt.

"What?" asked Kat.

"His Seecher Key. Where is it?" Tallia continued.

The Seechers all looked at each other.

"What's a Seecher Key?" Maya asked.

Sel thought for a moment.

"If we presume he entered the building via the Oneiri, as any of us probably would have done, he could have been funnelled into some sort of trap, forced to re-enter into the Skia. However, that would suggest they were aware of his presence. If I remember correctly, the great tragedy of the Paris Coupe of 1912 saw thirty-seven Seechers killed. This was a direct result of a tool that could detect Seechers in the Oneiri. It was a sort of tracking device, one that was originally invented by the Tauredunum."

"I would be very careful of entering their building in the Oneiri, if this is the case," Pep said as Sel agreed. Aris listened intently, whilst Maya looked completely lost.

"Sorry, what's the Oneiri?" She was met with a room full of blank faces, which frustrated her greatly. "Okay fine, don't tell me. Look. They have this whole secret project about finding Seechers. I know you can't tell me anything because I'm banned from knowing, but please! When was the last time any of you heard or saw him? Because if you thought he was with me, I haven't seen him for four days?! They have him. I saw it. We need to do something! Right now! Before he dies!" Maya rose to her feet and banged her fists on Pep's desk.

"Maya, please try and remain calm. We believe you. We're looking into it right now. We need you to stay here where you're safe with Aris and the other Potentials," Tallia said as she gestured for Aris to take Maya to the kitchen.

"So, you're going to go in there and save him. Now?! He's being kept on the ninth floor!" Maya demanded.

"Trust us. We'll do what we must," Pep replied.

Aris and Maya made their way to the kitchen. As soon as they left the room the door closed, and Pep ordered Tallia and Kat to go into the Oneiri and watch the Curative building from the outside only. He then instructed Sel to prepare some tactical plans to rescue Adam, whilst he would go and discuss it with the other Elders and finally provide them with the location of the new threat and all the information they'd now put together.

Aris and Maya entered the kitchen. Abi and Thomas had left. Maya was so fraught with emotion that when she threw herself into a chair, she accidently knocked a glass on the table, which smashed into the metal fruit bowl. Glass shattered across the reflective table surface. "Maya! Calm down. This isn't helping. The Seechers will get him back," Aris said.

"They said they're looking into it. That's hardly what I'd call urgent action. He looks awful. He's dying!" Maya shouted.

Aris moved closer to Maya. "Maya, please. We can't do anything right now. Let the Seechers do their job. Trust me, they'll rescue your dad. He'll be back here soon."

Maya pushed Aris away, "I left the office building as soon as I saw the footage and called you. I should've just stayed there and tried to get him out myself. Why did I leave? He's in there alone. God knows what they're doing to him!" Maya said as she got out of the chair and paced the room.

Aris picked up the broken glass.

"I have to go back. I can't stand being here, knowing he's in so much pain!" Maya said.

Aris looked up at her. He wasn't paying attention and accidently cut his finger on the large shard of glass he was holding in his hand.

"Shit!" Aris said as he dropped the shard back onto the table and sucked his wound.

"Are you okay?" Maya asked. A drop of Aris's blood left on the shard, slowly dripped onto the table.

"I'm fine, it's just a cut," Aris assured her. Maya started pacing and talking, but Aris's attention was drawn to where his blood had hit the tabletop. It was small, but the surface rippled in much the same way as he'd seen the mirror do when Pep threw a small drop of Epsilon on it, to open the gateway into the Oneiri. Aris leaned in closer.

"I know that building the best. I'm the one with access to it. They don't suspect anything about me. I'm just a stupid little fucking intern. God, I'm so stupid. This is all my fault. I'm going back in," Maya carried on, not noticing Aris's distraction.

Aris put his index finger to the ripple and, sure enough, it passed through the surface. He instantly recalled his conversation with Pep, about how his Epsilon was in his blood.

"I don't need a Seecher Key. I have my blood. Why have I never noticed this before?" Aris whispered.

"What?" Maya said. Aris pulled his finger back out, remembering how short gateways to the Oneiri remain open for.

"Maya, you can't go, it's too dangerous. What if they kidnap you, too? You have to stay here where it's safe." Aris went back to instinctively sucking on his wound.

"I'm going! Alone if I have to. If you come, I can get you in. Aris, you can help me. They'll think you're just another intern," Maya said, looking him in the eye.

"Fine, we'll go in together. But if it gets too dangerous, we leave," Aris said. Maya nodded.

"Is there a suit you could wear?"

———

"Take this badge," Maya said as she met Aris at the main entrance.

"How did you get this?" Aris asked as they walked through the restricted access door, in a suit that was clearly too large for him.

"I jumped onto the boss's computer. He's got a card programming device right there. But I'll need to update them to give us access to the security level. That's where dad is," Maya said as she strode down the corridor.

Maya ran into the office, shouting there was a fire on the security level and the whole room filtered out in about two minutes flat. She then locked the main door, and Aris pulled a desk in front of it. Now, she and Aris were alone in the office. Maya jumped on Simon's computer to update the cards.

"It might be a good idea to download some of the information so Pep and the others can work out what they're up to," Aris said as Maya handed him his updated access card.

"Fine. Do it on my computer in case anyone comes in here," Maya said as she finished updating her own card.

The two walked over to Maya's desk, where she quickly gained access to the server, she'd seen her dad on. She brought up the CCTV. Her dad looked terrible; he was hunched forward and his skin was sallow.

"He looks exactly like I saw him in my dream," Aris said.

Maya hit a few keys and his vital signs popped up on the screen. His heart rate was over a hundred and fifty and his blood pressure was very low. This prompted Maya to search the records. She quickly found a security log detailing her dad's capture and what had occurred since. Both Aris and Maya quickly read that after Dr Rivers took his Seecher Key from him, he became unwell. Over the last couple of days, his condition had taken a turn for the worse. There was reference to the fact that if he didn't get his Key, he would soon die. This brought tears to Maya's eyes.

"That's what the Seechers didn't want to tell us," she said. Aris looked panicked.

"Where's his Key then?" Aris probed.

"I'll search for some reference to it."

Searching the server even deeper, Maya brought up images of a locked room near Adam's location. In that room was his empty Seecher Key and something that appeared strange, but oddly familiar, to Aris. It was the glass hard drive.

"What's that?" Aris asked, pointing to the glass hard drive, the one he had seen himself holding on the rooftop so many times in his dreams.

Maya quickly brought up the schematics and description. It stated it was a hard drive that, when connected to a satellite system, would be able to locate every Seecher and Potential Seecher in the world. They both gasped at the sheer scale and horror of what that meant. Their dismay intensified when they read they planned to carry out the test within an hour.

"We need to get that drive, Maya. We need to get it now. We can't let them do this to the Seechers," Aris implored.

"Agreed. We need to get my dad's Key and get him out of here and take the drive," Maya replied. Just before they got up to leave, the door rattled. Simon's voice could be heard, "Open this door! Who's in there? I'm getting the other key."

Maya and Aris looked at each other wide-eyed. Maya glanced down at the final paragraph. "Wait, it says here they're going to return the Key to my dad after the scan tonight. They want to question him after, so they're going to keep him alive." Aris searched the room for something reflective.

"We need to get that hard drive now before it's connected to the satellite," Aris said as he picked up a pen knife on Simon's desk and re-cut the wound in his finger.

"Oh, my gosh! What are you doing?!" Maya gasped.

Aris didn't have time to answer. Simon had returned and unlocked the door. "Who's in there? Open this door now," he bellowed, pushing at the door, the desk in front of it holding it shut.

She worked on the system for a few moments, hacking in to shut down all the CCTV cameras in the security wing. "Clever!" Maya said as she looked up to see Aris smear his blood over the black mirrored surface of the largest TV screen in the room. The surface rippled.

"HEY! Come now, trust me," Aris shouted at her in a loud whisper. Maya ran to grab his hand and Aris yanked the two of them into the Oneiri.

They disappeared into the screen a fraction of a second before Simon and a few other men pushed the door so hard that the desk flew into the room and crashed on its side.

"There's no one in here," one of the men said, running into the room, gun raised. Aris and Maya watched from the Oneiri.

"Just come," Aris whispered to her, taking her hand, leading her out of the room.

The corridors were filled with security personnel, and Aris explained they couldn't see or hear them, but they had to wait for doors to be opened. It wasn't long before they had made it to the security wing and raced down the corridor.

At the security desk, the young face of the security guard was screwed up in confusion as a screen brought up a schematic of the building. On it, in Dr Rivers's department, a small yellow dot blinked. "What in Jupiter is that?"

It was early evening, and the daylight had faded. They followed a scientist into the artefacts' storeroom where Adam's Key and the glass hard drive were last seen on the CCTV.

Aris saw a large mirror in the room, smeared his blood on it, and they both entered back into the Skia. The scientist had his back turned, completing some final touches to the hard drive, as the two reappeared quietly into the room.

"Where are you going with that?" Maya demanded.

He nearly jumped out of his skin. "Sorry, I didn't hear you come in."

"I said, where are you taking that?" Maya demanded again.

"To the lab. Why? Who are you?" the scientist replied.

"Dr Rivers has sent us to find out exactly what you've been doing. They've been waiting. Here, let me take it," Maya said.

The scientist put the hard drive down and turned to face Maya directly.

"Let me call Dr Pine and check. What's your name?"

"Maya." As soon as the scientist turned to walk towards the phone, Maya picked up a large tray from the table and brought it smashing down on his head, knocking him clean out.

"Grab the hard drive, I'm going to get my dad's Key," Maya barked.

"You're scary," Aris said as he quickly picked up the hard drive.

"And you just made me disappear?! Let's not judge each other!" Maya remarked back.

As he held the glass device in his hands, the blue light drew him in, and the memory of his dream, of him holding the hard drive before, replayed in his mind. "Maya, this has your dad's Epsilon in it. They've taken the Epsilon out of your dad's Key, I guess to power this hard drive. He needs the Epsilon more than anything. This is his essence, his life force."

"Okay, we'll just give him both," Maya replied.

"Maya, wait. I'm going to tell you something, and you need to trust me. I know what I'm going to say may seem weird, and it will involve you doing something you said you would never do, but I need you to." Aris's heart raced.

Maya eyed him as she placed her dad's empty Seecher Key into her pocket. The Epsilon from his Key resided inside the hard drive.

"What?"

"I don't know how, or exactly why, but before this night is over, we'll find ourselves on the roof. You'll aim a gun at me. Remember that dream I told you about? Where you shoot me. It's today. And it needs to happen. I know it. When we're on the roof, you need to pull that trigger, right at me." Maya took a long, deep breath in. Aris continued solemnly, "It's the only way to save your dad and all the other Seechers, that's why he said, you can save us all. If these guys use this device, they'll know where every Seecher in the world is, and if they get that information, they'll be after all of us. We can't let them have that drive. We really can't. What the Seechers do is far more important than I can even begin to explain to you right now. But you have to trust me. Pep told me my Epsilon runs through my blood, that's why I can make a gateway to the Oneiri, and that's why I won't die when you shoot me. When you pull that trigger, everything will be fine," Aris finished.

Maya stared back.

"Oh, my God! Aris? I can't shoot you?!" she replied.

"You can, Maya, and you must. How do we get out of here?" he asked.

"Put his lab coat on. And hide this under it. Time's running short."

Aris took the lab coat off the scientist and put it on, then he stuffed the blue glowing hard drive underneath it.

———

Trying to find where Adam was, the two found themselves enter a ward area that was part of the medical wing. Though they soon wished they hadn't. With nauseating shock, they recognized their old university friend, Stephen Monroe. He was totally motionless, looking gaunt and vacant, with his head shaved, in a white hospital gown, staring at a blank wall.

He was in a room full of similar-looking young adults with their heads shaved, dressed in hospital gowns. A line of dribble came from the corner of his mouth, his skin drained of all colour. They rushed over to Stephen and tried to talk to him. Sadly, he made no response. Aris and Maya noticed a huge scar on the back of his head. They all had scars. Aris pulled Maya away.

"What the fuck?" Maya said with tears in her eyes.

Aris took her hands in his and tried to refocus her. "We can't help them right now. We need to find your dad! Immediately!"

Aris gulped as he suddenly found himself face to face with the young woman that he'd dreamt about being abducted in the streets of Oxford.

"What is it?" Maya asked.

"It's nothing" Aris tugged her away.

They left that sickening place and, a short time later, they reached the corridor where her father's cell was. Carefully peeking around the corner, they caught a glimpse of three security guards and a doctor outside the door.

"We need to take him to the medical wing. He needs care before he gets his Key back. Dr Rivers will kill us if he dies on us," a doctor said to the security guards. The doctor put his finger to his ear as he listened to a radio earpiece.

"Hang on. There's an announcement on the internal radios. Apparently, there's more Seechers in the building. Okay we'd better take him now," the doctor instructed.

"Shit. They're moving him," Maya said as she pushed Aris back against the wall to make sure they were both out of view.

"We need to keep this out of their hands," Aris said, gesturing to the drive under his coat. "We should leave now and get the Seechers to come back for your dad."

"No, he's not going to last that long! We should follow them. We can give him the Key and that thing, and he can regain his power and get us out," Maya said.

"Maya, he's too weak. We don't know if he'll recover quickly enough with his empty Key, and I don't know how to get the Epsilon out of this thing and back into his Key! All we do know is that they plan to use this to hunt down all the Seechers in the world. We need to get this as far away from them as possible so they can't do that," Aris replied.

"No. We can't leave him. I can't lose him. He means more to me than the bloody Seechers." Maya gritted her teeth.

"Maya, you're not thinking straight. We can't let them do that scan. The Seechers will get here before anything happens trust me. We need to leave now," Aris pleaded.

Maya glared at him, "I can't lose my dad. I'm not losing both my parents, Aris. How can I leave him here to die? And if we take that now, he will."

"Okay. Why don't we go back to your office and make a plan? It's too much of a risk to follow these guys right now. We can find out where they're taking him and go from there. People are starting to look at us," Aris said, trying to placate her.

"Okay. Maybe. What about Simon?"

The two made their way back to Maya's office. They were just getting near when Aris noticed a stairwell, which was signposted for the roof. Maya was walking purposefully ahead. It was the ideal opportunity for Aris to slip off the lab coat, put the hard drive under his arm and race up the stairs.

As Maya entered the office, she turned to speak to Aris, but he was gone. Her eyes caught a glimpse of the stairwell's door just swinging closed, and she instantly knew.

She heard the heavy footsteps of a security team walking up the corridor outside. Looking around the office, Maya composed herself, brushing her hair back with her hands and pulling her blazer straight, she walked past the other workers. Simon wasn't there. Maya casually crouched next to his desk and forcibly opened his drawer.

———

"STOP!" Maya's voice sounded exactly the same as he'd remembered from his dream.

Aris turned to see Maya standing behind him as he reached the roof's edge. The words left his lips as though it was a script he'd learnt. "Maya."

"I can't believe this is *really* happening," Maya spoke, her voice trembling, gun in hand.

"The others will be here soon. There's still time to make this right."

Aris knew what she had to do.

"Aris, please. You have to give it back. This means more to me than it does to you!"

"I can't! How many others are going to die if this carries on?! I can't let this happen. I'm sorry, Maya." Aris edged back as he spoke. The drop was behind him. It was like clockwork. Security men were soon right behind Maya.

"Give me the hard drive!" Maya shouted. Her eyes filled with tears.

"I forgive you," Aris said as Dr Rivers moved to Maya's side.

"That hard drive's property of Curative Analytical. You're trespassing and stealing. I'm not sure what business you have here…"

Aris zoned out briefly.

The gun fired.

Sharp, excruciating pain spread from his back and stretched throughout his entire body. It was an agony he had never felt before. The pain overrode everything as he fell forwards. Headfirst. Soaring down the thirteen stories.

A Glimpse into the Beyond

Large droplets of blood raced ahead of Aris's falling figure. When the blood fused with the surface of the river, a flash of barely distinguishable blue, shimmered just ahead of his near-lifeless body. It had made a portal into the Oneiri, right before he plunged into the surface of the river.

Ice cold water brought Aris around. He flapped and flailed about, trying to reach the surface. As he breached the water, he took in a large gulp of air.

Aris struggled to remain conscious. The chill had become unbearable, and his back screamed in immeasurable pain. He could see the bank of the river and realised he wouldn't last long if he didn't get out of the water.

With all the energy he had, he headed for the side. A loud *splash* resonated behind him. He didn't turn to look at what caused it but, instantly, he felt arms wrap around and hold him high in the water. Swimming was easier. He was suddenly moving faster. Soon, he was at the bank and clambering onto dry land, thanks to his unknown helper.

Rolling on to his side, he felt overwhelming relief. His vision blurred as a woman's silhouette stood over him.

"Be careful, Aris, they seek only to control you." He knew her voice.

It was the same woman who called him into the lift before he was attacked at the hospital. Aris squinted hard to try and distinguish her features but, before he could make anything out, she was gone.

In the distance, Aris heard footsteps race towards him.

"He's not in the Skia, Kat, he's in the Oneiri," Tallia exclaimed as she touched Aris's arm.

Kat's knelt to inspect his wounds. "He's been shot in the stomach and is losing a lot of blood."

"I need wormwood, or iron wood. A strong healing energy," Tallia said as she rose to her feet to look around at the plant life. She took a few steps away, and then shouted, "Tyche." Waves of energy lit up the night.

"Aris, stay with me," Kat said as she rolled up his shirt to see the bullet wound.

Tallia returned. Her hands full with glowing sapphire light. As she lowered herself, she returned the Oneiri back to normal colour, concealing the other waves.

"This should stabilize you." Tallia said as she pressed the glowing light into the wounds on his back and stomach. Barely conscious, Aris could feel a warm sensation that eased some of his pain.

"It will stop some of the internal bleeding. But there's still a lot of damage," Tallia said, looking at Kat.

Aris moved his hands and held up the blue glowing hard drive, to Tallia.

"It's Adam's Epsilon, he needs it. He's dying," Aris said, his voice barely audible.

Tallia took the strange object from Aris and inspected it.

"Take him back to the guild, Kat. I'm going in to get Adam," Tallia said, as she turned to face the building behind her. There was a lot of commotion unfolding around them in the Skia. A helicopter beamed light down onto the river. Boats converged around the spot where Aris had entered the Oneiri. Divers jumped into the water, searching for what Tallia now had in her hand.

Kat watched in dismay for a moment. Tallia placed the hard drive deep inside her coat and made her way towards a nearby bus stop. Flicking some of her own Epsilon onto a reflective glass pane, Tallia stepped through into the Skia. Once through, she dropped some Epsilon from her Key onto her hand. She rubbed her hands together and stretched them wide.

Suddenly, out of the darkness of night, obsidian urban foxes padded softly into view under a streetlight. Their matted fur rose, and their sharp teeth bared. At the same time, a flock of starlings, like blacker shadows against a black sky, swooped in and danced above Tallia, their wings beating hard, eyes glinting mad. Her Aeon army had assembled.

———

Dr Rivers peered back over the edge. He could see nothing of the strange young man.

"Mark, Simon, ensure that the building is completely secured. Get the other helicopter down here now, launch more boats and divers. Anything to find that hard drive." As the doctor yelled his orders, he turned to look back at Maya, lost amongst the armed guards. "Take that gun off her. You did well for acting so quickly." Maya was frozen to the core as a guard prised the gun from her clenched hand. "Does anyone know where he came from?" Maya shook her head.

"Doctor, I have urgent news from Dr Clements. She says the captive Seecher has become critically unstable, and she fears he won't survive the night. She's recommending he be taken to a hospital," the red-faced PA said as he rushed up to this boss, showing an iPad screen. Maya looked at the screen for a brief second, gritting her teeth.

Dr Rivers took the tablet and made his way off the roof. Others followed. Maya stayed alone in the moonlight, trembling from head to toe.

Dr Rivers walked down the concrete stairwell, followed by his staff. They entered a main corridor.

"Call her. Tell her to keep him there. Keep him alive. We'll have his Epsilon returned within a couple hours, once we've salvaged it." He passed the iPad back to him and continued onwards.

A door off the corridor opened, and Mark emerged. "Sir, boats are out. Helicopter two is coming. I'm about to—" Before he could finish, lights in the corridor turned red, and an alarm rang out.

"Report!" Rivers barked at the PA.

He raised the iPad and tapped rapidly on the screen.

"I am getting reports of… Animals in the building. The emergency evacuation order has been given," he said, scrunching up his face.

"What?! Absurd. Overrun that order. Now!"

"I can't, sir. The order has come from the directors," he muttered.

"No. Surely not. Let me see that." He snatched the iPad out of his hands.

Dr Rivers tapped the screen hard.

"Bastards," Rivers breathed out, slamming the iPad back into the PA's chest.

"Mark, get down the stairs and lock the Seecher down. I don't want him moved. No one is to relocate him." Dr Rivers punched the wall, then marched down the corridor alone.

"You backstabbing bastard," Dr Rivers shouted as he burst into Mielikki 's office. Two office staff carrying boxes jumped when the door swung open. Mielikki was at his desk, placing items into a box.

"Come in, why don't you." Professor Mielikki's face was stony cold. He looked to the staff. "You two, load those items and make sure all medical personnel are ready to leave within thirty minutes."

As soon as the two had left, Dr Rivers closed the door. "You told the directors. Don't deny it. The only person outside my team who knew was Clements, and she told you. And you told the directors."

Mielikki calmly placed the last few items into the box. "Don't storm in here, throwing allegations at me. Dr Clements did come to me to discuss your captive Seecher's health. She divulged the information whilst Dr Foster was in the room. I would suspect he is the source of the disclosure."

"Bastard," Dr Rivers said as the professor walked towards him.

"They had the right to know. It was your mistake to not inform them straight away."

"I was going to. Once I knew where all the Seechers were located," Dr Rivers breathed out.

"This weakness of yours. This inexhaustible craving for recognition and reward has inevitably become your downfall." Mielikki paused. "Goodbye, Rivers. You're an impressive man. Just don't let your ambitions destroy you. Hopefully when the units are reunified, you'll still be with the company." He smiled slyly and left his office, carrying a box of belongings. Dr Rivers stood in the empty office for a few moments longer, contemplating his words.

———

The entrance to the building opened, and the two security guards rose to their feet in surprise. Tallia strode in confidently as starlings screamed past her head, flying on, down the corridor. The stealthy pack of foxes trotted around her sides, leaping onto the tables. Security guards reached for their holstered guns. Tallia had a small blue marble bag in her right hand.

She delved inside the bag, pulling out two seeds. She rubbed them between her fingers, and then cast them at the men. As the two grains spun in the air, they glowed an Epsilon blue. Nearing the men, the seeds burst open, and reams of vines sprung forth. The lianas wrapped around the guards, imprisoning them. Tallia moved over to the security desk and quickly searched through the computer. Another guard rushed into the lobby, but before he could react to the odd sight before him, the foxes were upon him, clawing and biting.

"They're in the medical wing." As Tallia shouted, alarm bells rang out, and the screen in front of her flashed with bold red.

Evacuation order – activated.

She exited the lobby in the direction of where she believed Adam to be. Her course was swarmed with people as security and office staff vacated the building.

The birds now flew throughout the lower levels. Having located Adam, they had returned to guide Tallia towards him. Two guards were outside the medical department. Tallia disabled them with the throw of a seed, entangling them with fast-growing strangle vines.

Barging into the medical ward, Tallia's eyes instantly fell upon Adam. A tall, blonde woman was in the middle of giving him CPR, blowing into his mouth and pumping his chest.

"Adam!" Tallia raced to his side. "Step back," she commanded.

"It's too late. He's dead," Dr Clements cried.

Tallia turned to look at her. Then stretched out her arm and touched the stranger's chest. Dr Clements dropped to the floor. Tallia pressed her hands against Adam's chest. Her hands glowed blue, as the last of the Epsilon on her hands began to channel some of her own life energy, into him.

Adam gasped deeply for air.

"Adam," she screamed. Feeling a little faint from the transfer, Tallia wrenched the hard drive out, and placed it on his chest. "Rule one, always keep your Epsilon close."

It glowed even more brightly, as Adam breathed in and out.

———

"The wound goes right through him. I've encouraged the cells to begin the healing of the tissues and muscles. Luckily, there's no major organ damage. I think, with a bit of rest, he'll be back on his feet in a few weeks," Tallia said as she placed a dressing over the front and back of Aris's wounds while talking to Kat.

Aris awoke in the Seechers' medical room.

"Where's Maya?" he muttered.

"Maya?" Kat asked, frowning.

"Yes, is she here? Did you save her dad?"

"Adam's here, and he's doing just fine. What do you mean, where's Maya?"

"She was in the building. Did you get her out, too?"

"What? Oh, no," Kat said, her jaw dropping.

"I had to leave her behind. She might still be there!" Aris spoke as he tried to lift himself in the bed.

———

A helicopter flew over the London night skyline. Inside was Dr Rivers, Simon, Mark and Maya Green. She was gagged, and her hands were bound. On his iPad, Dr Rivers showed her CCTV footage of her and Aris disappearing into the large TV screen moments before Simon and his men pushed the desk out of the way of the door.

Maya remained still. Tears ran from her eyes as her heart pounded.

"So, it seems our little protégée is working for both sides." Dr Rivers whispered.

"Whilst I was in the Oneiri, I found myself trapped in this small mirrored room. My only option was to return to the Skia. I tried to bend the Kairos Reflection around the door. Which I did, but then I was incapacitated by some form of Epsilac electricity. I collapsed. When I awoke, my Key was gone. They interrogated me, but I said very little. Though it was obvious they already knew a lot about us. They have Tauredunum technology and wanted to know how we extracted a pure form of Epsilon, which they are unable to do. They can only get Epsilac. We should hit them now and hit them hard," Adam finished talking, his head and wounds well-bandaged. Pep and Sel listened intently.

"We'll strike in the morning. Seechers from Paris, Amsterdam, and Munich will join us then," Pep replied.

"Tallia reported that they were in the process of evacuating the building," Sel said.

"Then we shall go as soon as the others arrive," Pep confirmed.

Tallia burst into the room.

"We have a problem." She paused as she looked straight at Adam. "It's Maya. She was in the building with Aris, but she hasn't returned."

"Oh, God. No," Adam uttered, his voice trembling. "Are you sure?"

"Yes, Aris has just woken up. He told me that they broke in there together last night. It was Maya who shot him." They all looked stunned.

"Really?" Adam asked.

"Yes. As far as we know, she's still in there," Tallia said.

"Then we can't wait, we need to go now," Sel said, standing tall.

"Agreed. Four of us will go. Tallia, you stay with Aris. Adam, Sel, Kat, and I will launch the attack," Pep proposed, to which they all agreed.

Aris rose from the bed. He couldn't sleep, despite how many times Tallia protested he must. He was so worried about Maya and felt completely helpless.

"Slow down Aris, your wound's very fragile. You risk doing more damage if you keep moving around like that," Tallia said as she came into the room, seeing the young man pacing about.

"Ah. God damn it. I need to be out there helping," Aris shouted, through gritted teeth, the pain was almost unbearable. His hand moved to rest over the dressing.

"Is there any more pain relief?"

"You've had all you can, for now. Sit down and show some patience. I'll see if I can ease any more for you," Tallia said as she pointed to the bed.

Aris perched on the edge as Tallia moved towards him. She took out her Key. Tallia reluctantly dropped more Epsilon onto her hands and proceeded to drift them over his wounds. A cold, soothing sensation rushed through Aris's body, and the pain subsided.

"Thank you, that's a lot better," Aris said as Tallia finished.

"You still need to rest!"

"How do you do that exactly? I mean, how do you control the power of your Epsilon? You know, to make it do what you want it to do?" Aris asked.

Tallia gazed at Aris.

"Control over the power of Epsilon is all within the mind. Deep focus and concertation. These are the fundamentals of the early Potential training. Understanding the very Reflection you want to manipulate. Fathoming it out, and clearly instructing the Epsilon with your thought and will."

"So, you think of what you want, and the Epsilon does it?" Aris surmised.

"Sort of, Aris. You are very peculiar. You know that don't you. These are things you'll learn in time, with the others, when you train. You and the other Potentials will soon start the Seecher trials, once all this mess is behind us. The trials are designed, not only to test if you're ready for the activation tank, but also to help you develop the skills you need to manipulate the Reflection you'll specialise in when you're a Seecher. But you don't need to think about using the power until you've undergone the activation. It's important that only those who are truly ready should use their power. Both in the Skia and in the Oneiri, the power can cause great harm if not taught properly. I take it you're smart enough to see that?" Tallia explained.

"I do. Sorry to bombard you. I just want to help Maya so badly. I feel like it's all my fault," Aris replied.

"None of this is your fault. None of it. This is the world we live in. This is why we operate in secret. And right now, the best thing you can do for Maya is…" Tallia stopped and looked up as Sel opened the door.

"The place was empty. Tallia, come with me, please," he said.

"There was nothing there. No people, no computers, no files. I've never known a building to be vacated so quickly. It was seriously as though no one had ever been there before," Sel said. Tallia, Kat, and Pep were the only ones listening. Adam sat in the corner with his head in his hands.

"So, what next? They must have left something we can follow?" Tallia asked.

"They've done a good job. I think it might be worth you heading over and seeing if you can manipulate the Aeon Reflection to see if there are any hidden traces on it," Pep suggested to Tallia as he glanced sympathetically to Adam.

"I'll go with you," Kat said. Sel quickly offered to join them, and the three got up to make their way back. When they left the room, Pep went over to Adam.

"We'll find her, Adam. I promise. Before the night's out."

"I can't lose her, Pep." Adam sobbed.

"We're going to find her. We're Seechers. And we'll bring our enemy to justice. You have my word."

Aris felt himself getting more and more worked up. As his unease increased, so did the sharp stabbing pain in his wound. He knew his movements were agitating it, but he couldn't stop himself.

"I *have* to do something," he said aloud. No one replied.

He paced a few more times until the wound on his back sent out a pain so piercing it made his legs shake. He placed a hand to the wound and could feel the sticky wetness of blood seep through the dressing. Lifting his hand, he stared at the blood before he walked to the mirror and raised his shirt up to inspect how much blood had soaked through to his front.

He stared into his reflection and contemplated what he knew and what he could do. His power, was his blood. Then, with determination on his face, Aris ripped off the dressings, placed his hands over his wounds, and focused his thoughts solely on healing them. He poured all his concentration, will and might into it and, as he did, a strange tingling sensation resonated within.

The pain momentarily increased, but he was certain he could feel himself healing faster. After several agonising minutes, he removed his hands and was astonished to see there was no more exposed tissue, just pink, healthy skin. It was swollen and tender, but the wounds had completely closed.

"Holy shit," he uttered, lifting his blood-stained hands. "It really is in my blood."

"It's your Key."

The woman's voice startled Aris. He suddenly looked back at the mirror, as that's where the voice came from. His reflection had disappeared. Stood opposite him, looking at him with soft eyes, was the woman who had mysteriously aided him several times before.

"Who are you?" he asked stepping closer.

"I'm here to help you."

Aris stared at her. She looked different from before. She had a scar across her left eye, and her left cheek was bruised.

"Help me. Help me find Maya," he ordered.

"Aris, you don't need my help to find her. You just need to let go."

Aris studied her appearance. She was middle-aged, blonde, her eyes green and, despite her bruised face, she was beautiful.

"Let go?" he asked.

She lifted her hand up, then faced the palm towards him. He could see a cut, with blood dripping from it.

"The Oneiri is yours to control, to create. Let go and embrace your destiny."

Aris raised his hand, matching her movement and, as his fingertips touched hers on the hard surface of the mirror, she vanished. Aris pulled his hand away, expecting to see his own reflection return, but it didn't. Instead, it appeared as though he was watching a live video feed, of sorts.

He could make out several men and women moving boxes and crates around. He could make out some small aeroplanes through the open doors of a hangar in the background. His eyes then fell upon Maya. She was handcuffed to a chair, just off the centre of what he could see.

"Maya!" he shouted in vain.

He touched the mirror frantically, thinking it might be a gateway, but it wasn't. His eyes swept about, trying to distinguish features. He spotted a sign resting on the top of a doorway.

- *Bourn Airfield.*

"Holy shit," Aris said. He paused for a second before darting out of the room to head towards the Seechers.

———

Aris was sat in the Plato's Oculus, the glass balls above him, playing out his memory of the airfield and Maya in it. Pep paced about.

"We must go now," he demanded, taking the helmet off Aris.

"Pep, we can't base a mission on Aris's vision alone," Tallia said. Kat came in, still putting the final touches on to her Seecher battle outfit.

It isn't too dissimilar from some kind of traditional ninja garment, Aris thought.

"Tallia, I appreciate what you're saying, but we have no other leads. And Adam will go without us, anyway."

"She's there, Tallia. I know she is," Aris pleaded.

Adam and Sel walked into the room, both dressed in their battle wear. Sel held a strange silk bag that fitted nicely in his palm. He made his way to Tallia and handed it to her.

"It's done. We can't waste any more time," Sel insisted.

"Let's go," Pep relayed as Kat, Sel, and Adam swiftly left the room. Pep followed. Tallia rushed to his side.

"Are you sure I should stay here?" she asked.

"Someone needs to protect the guild and the Potentials. And we need your help with our exit," Pep replied.

"Why take Aris with you? It could be dangerous," Tallia whispered as the pair neared the Mirror Room.

"He'll be safe. He'll stay in the Oneiri. We need him to confirm the airfield."

They turned the corner, and in front of them was a rippling mirror. Kat stood next to Aris.

"Sel and Adam are on the other side," Kat said to Pep.

"I'm amazed you've healed yourself like that Aris. But are you sure you're ready to enter the Oneiri again?" Tallia worried.

"As long as I don't get shot," Aris quipped.

"We'll watch out for you," Kat said as she stepped through the gateway.

"Tallia, I'll be fine. Thank you for all your help," Aris said as he, too, stepped through.

"We will return with Maya. I know it." Pep nodded before he, too, disappeared.

<hr />

Travelling through Oneiri wasn't like making one's way in the Skia. Not for a Seecher. As well as the rules that governed what can and cannot be passed through, there was also the ability to travel great distances in almost the blink of eye, as long as you didn't pass through a dense concentration of the substance Reflection, what the Seechers call Hyle.

It was a skill that required mastery, much like the knowledge and capability to bend the Reflection in the real world. Pep had accelerated their passage through the Oneiri by taking control of their movement and guiding them, expertly and rapidly, through the streets of London and to the outskirts of the city. As space warped around them, the four Seechers and Aris came to a halt on a grass verge, looking down towards the airfield.

Big green hangars and a few other smaller buildings filled their vision. It seemed very familiar to Aris. Even down to the detail of the commotion of vehicles and people, darting around. The hangar doors were exactly the same as what he'd seen earlier in the mirror.

"That was amazing," Aris said, holding his side and catching his breath as he looked about.

"Over there. That's it. That's where Maya is. In through those hangar doors." Aris pointed.

"Seechers, you know what to do. Stay safe. Adam, neutralize all targets, secure Maya, and get her out of there. The rest of us will flank you and go in search for answers," Pep said as he turned to face the airfield.

"What about me?" Aris asked.

"You stay here, in the Oneiri. You're safe here. When Adam rescues Maya, he'll come back and take you and her to the guild," Pep finished. The four Seechers stepped forward in a line, side by side, glaring down at the airfield.

Aris watched the Seechers as they prepared to move. His attention was broken by a large kestrel which swooped down and hovered just in front of him. Tight in the grip of its claws was the silk bag that Sel had given Tallia. Releasing the bag from its talons, the kestrel swung in the air and sped away. The bag landed a few meters in front of the Seechers.

As the strappings loosened, the bag seemed to move. The top of it opened. Within it was a mound of sand. The grains expanded and multiplied, spilling out onto the ground. Aris watched in amazement as the grains organised themselves to stretch upwards. Within a short space of time, there was a wall of sand in front of them.

It was huge. Six-foot-high by six foot wide. Suddenly, it glowed a deep red, as though it was being heated by an unseen force. Aris with an amazed expression turned towards Sel.

"I imprinted the manipulation whilst at the guild, before I gave it to Tallia. Another skill you may master one day." Sel said as he winked at Aris.

The redness faded. What was speckled sand moments before was now morphing into a shining, perfectly glistening mirror.

"Good job," Kat exclaimed as they approached the mirror. Sel smiled.

Pep took out his Key and flicked some of his Epsilon against the Mirror. It rippled as the doorway between two worlds, once again opened.

"Wait here. I'll be back for you," Adam said to Aris as the four Seechers entered the Skia.

Aris watched as the Seechers made their way towards the buildings. He stepped forward. He felt he should follow them.

How will they know if I wait here or follow them? he thought. *I'll go, too, but remain in the Oneiri. I'm safe inside here where no one can see me.*

Aris quickly caught up with the Seechers and watched first-hand as they burst onto the grounds of the airfield and launched an attack.

Sel was the first to engage the enemies. He altered the fabric of their clothes to a heavy lead and they fell to the ground, laden under the weight. Pep used his powers to force large objects that lay about, to hit unsuspecting guards. He also picked up and flung a few more guards sideways as they raced towards them. Adam halted time around other guards and workers, who suddenly froze still like mannequins. One man managed to dodge his Kairos Reflection manipulation, but Adam just punched him to the ground instead, releasing his rage. Kat used her gift to make eight guards drop unconscious before her. She also projected illusions into a group of about ten men's minds, hypnotising them to believe they were hopelessly alone and forgotten. They curled up and forgot about the fight, too wrapped up in their own despair.

The Seechers' initial attack had taken the guards by complete surprise and, within a matter of minutes, thirty guards lay on the floor, incapacitated.

Dr Rivers heard the shouts and commotion of the attack from the hangar he was in. Looking out of a window, he saw the Seechers continue their onslaught, making their way towards him.

"Get your batons, we're under attack. Simon, get all men to the main hangar. Hold them off. Mark prepare the paraphernalia," the Dr bellowed his orders as he picked up his own baton and raced down a set of stairs. As he reached the ground, multitudes of guards raced past him to exit the building and engage the Seechers.

In the open arena outside, the Seechers met the resistance. The guards with batons fired glowing yellow projectiles at the Seechers, who dived for cover. Some guards extended their batons to the size of baseball bats and tried to strike the Seechers as they ran.

The Seechers were unrelenting in their attack, manipulating the Reflections. Pep sent four of them, flying. Sel turned the ground to quicksand as guard after guard fell into the sinking trap. Kat continued to cast illusions into their minds, each one falling before her without getting a chance to strike. A large proportion of Rivers's men now lay unconscious, defeated. Adam glanced at the entrance to the hangar and darted off.

Kat noticed and quickly followed. She was soon joined by Sel and Pep.

Aris watched in amazement as the battle unfolded. In the Oneiri, he, too, followed into to the hangar.

The Seechers entered through the huge doors. At first, they saw no one in there. To one side of the room, there was an open door. Maya sat in a chair. Her face gleamed when she saw her father.

Adam ran to the room and quickly disintegrated the handcuffs on Maya's wrists. They shared a momentary embrace.

"We're not alone, there are more people here," Kat said, scanning and sensing them through the open palms of her hands.

Dr Rivers, Mark, and Simon were hidden in various locations in the hangar. Mark was in a cupboard, fiddling with a large square box covered with strange Greek symbols that glowed yellow. Simon lay behind a filing cabinet. In one hand he had his baton, in the other was a small pistol. Dr Rivers was sat some way away but was trapped by the Seechers congregating near the entrance.

Simon rushed out from behind the stack. Aiming his gun, he pulled the trigger.

Bullets flew at Pep, who instantly raised his hands, and the bullets deflected off an invisible field he conjured. With a flick of Pep's wrist, the gun exploded in Simon's hand.

At that moment, Dr Rivers rushed out and aimed his baton at Pep and fired a glowing yellow projectile. Pep didn't understand at first what it was. Reacting on instinct, he swung his hand in its direction. But, this time, the invisible field was powerless. Two metallic projectiles cut through the air and struck Pep in the chest. They sent a surge of electricity coursing through his body, and he fell to the floor in a spasm.

Sel saw this and reacted by transforming a nearby wall into a moving solid fluid. The wall came alive as it stretched out two tentacle-like arms, which wrapped around Dr Rivers's wrists and pulled them back against its surface before re-hardening again. Rivers was now not only trapped by these concrete handcuffs, but his feet were not even touching the ground. He dangled precariously in the air.

Kat moved over to Pep and removed the metal bolts as Pep yelped in pain. Aris watched this all unfold with his mouth wide. Before Aris could move, he saw a small, yellow, glowing box roll into view.

Adam walked back to the others, holding Maya by the hand. Both noticed the cube roll on the floor before it came to a halt. Sel moved his hands in the direction of the box, but nothing happened. Confusion crossed Sel's face.

"It's Tauredunum!" Sel yelled. Then, before any other Seecher could act, the box *clicked* loudly, sending out large yellow bursts of smoke in every direction.

The room quickly filled with smoke. Aris, watched as the air distorted and an arc of crackling electricity emanated from within the yellow cloud. It was more than just a smoke screen.

Pep limped a few steps, then waved his hand. But it was useless. Nothing happened. The thick yellow fog cancelled out their powers.

Now barely able to see more than half a foot in front of them, the sound of gunshots screamed through the air.

Mark aimed his gun into the yellow mist firing at random. The Seechers, concealed by the yellow cloud, dropped to the floor and clambered for cover. Simon quickly made his way to where he believed Dr Rivers was. On reaching him, he hit the constraints of the wall with his baton, breaking the brick. Soon, Rivers was free. He pulled out his gun, and he, too, mindlessly fired in the direction where he'd last seen Pep.

Aris stood with his hands on his face, helpless in the Oneiri. He saw the outline of the men firing. He could see the flashes of the howling bullets. He could see Sel behind a desk, struck with a bullet wound to his shoulder. Aris could also just about make out Maya and Adam, who'd taken refuge back to where she'd been tied up earlier. Aris needed to do something but didn't know what.

"They're in peril, Aris. You can help them. You just need to let go." The female voice came from behind him. The woman from the mirror now stood just in front of the entrance door. He could see her clearly.

"How?" he screamed, heart racing.

"Remember, Aris. The energy in here is yours to control, to create," she spoke, her eyes fixed on his.

Aris quickly grabbed a sharp stone from the floor and dug it deep into his palm. Blood pooled out of his hand. "Tyche," he shouted.

The entire hangar seemed to burst into light. It was a combination of browns and dirty blacks, all dull in colour. He stared down at his hand and concentrated his thoughts on positivity and good fortune. *They need luck,* he thought. Bright Jade green fog burst from his hand, which intensified, getting larger and larger. The warmth of it sent surges of ecstasy through his body. He gazed in wonder as the energy grew brighter and more intense. The sound of reloading guns jolted him back. He had to act.

He raised his hands high, and then dropped them to the ground. As the green light hit the floor, Aris watched as it billowed out and bathed the entire space in its jade hue. It washed over the Seechers, infusing them with Aris's good luck.

At the same moment, in the Skia, every door and window in the building swung open, and a peculiar and unexpected large gust of wind tore through. The swirling, intense flurry of air swept up the yellow fog in a matter of seconds and blew it straight out of the openings.

It all happened so quickly that those in the room didn't have time to adjust. Dr Rivers could see Kat lying on the floor as clear as day. He aimed his gun. Mark at his side, aimed his gun at the wounded Sel. Both men moments from pulling the trigger.

Pep spied the two men aim their weapons and launched his hands in their direction, sending out such a powerful force that it picked them both up and threw them out of the hangar doors.

Mark collided with the floor, rolling a few times before coming to a stop. Dr Rivers smashed hard into the side of a large metal container. Mark scurried over to the doctor. Mark grabbed Dr Rivers's arm as he wailed.

"We've lost," Mark said as he helped the doctor to his feet and briskly made their way to a car.

Pep struggled to pull himself up. Kat was quick to her feet and was soon at Sel's side, putting pressure on the wound.

"Oh my gosh. My shoulder!" Sel said as Kat helped him up. Adam and Maya walked back in to join them and helped the others up.

Aris watched the Seechers with a sigh of relief. He clutched at his hand, which still felt like it was on fire. Turning to the doorway, Aris's eyes widened. The woman still stood there.

"Who are you?" Aris quizzed.

"You need to find me, Aris. To find me is to know yourself."

He watched as an invisible force pulled her backwards through the door. He promptly followed her outside as the mysterious woman rose high into the air. Towards a bright white light. The woman disappeared from his vision.

———

Mark drove as fast as his car would allow. Racing the motorway at 140mph, he felt it would have been impossible for any of the Seechers to have followed them.

Soon, Mark pulled into a large warehouse. He parked the car and carried Dr Rivers out. Two security guards moved towards them. They had the same strange batons Dr Rivers's guards had.

"Excuse me, gentleman, this is private property. You need to leave," one of the guards ordered.

"Don't you know who this is?" Mark hissed.

"No. So, get back in the car and disappear." But before Dr Rivers or Mark could reply, the guard's radios went off. They both discretely turned to listen. After a few moments, the guard who'd spoken so directly, turned to Dr Rivers. "Apologies sir. Your admission has just been authorized. You'll be met in the reception area."

One guard stood to the side, whilst the other opened the main door to the warehouse. Mark and the injured Dr Rivers went through. They entered a small waiting area, with an unmanned reception desk. Professor Mielikki soon appeared.

"I'm incredibly surprised to see you here at this hour of the morning, Doctor, and in such a mess," the professor added, eyeing up the wounded doctor.

"We were attacked before we could depart. A group of Seechers overpowered us. We lost everything," Dr Rivers said, his voice fragile.

"Well, if you fly too close to the sun, you're bound to get burnt,"

Mielikki continued. "Why have you come here?"

Dr Rivers held his side. "Where else can we go?"

The professor let out an audible sigh. "How did you know where the medical evacuation site was? It was meant to be top secret."

"Internal espionage. I apologize. It's nothing personal. I found out where everyone's fallback was. Just in case I was unable to proceed from the airfield," Dr Rivers said.

"I appreciate your honesty. Airfield?" Dr Rivers squirmed as shots of pain surged through his side. "I shan't play games with you, Dr Rivers. My men had already told me about your interference on this. I was annoyed. But fear not. I didn't share it with the directors." Dr Rivers nodded in appreciation. "Come, I'll get your injuries seen to. Mark, I take it you took adequate precautions getting here? I certainly don't want any unexpected Seechers turning up."

"Of course. We weren't followed," Mark said.

"Good, then it's this way gentleman." Professor Mielikki led them through several doors and into the main workings of the building. They passed room after room of extraction sites where teenagers and young adults were strapped to trolleys. There was one large Nightingale ward space, with two long rows of beds filled with children softly crying, some hallucinating; all were broken.

Thomas and Abi had been worried sick about Maya. They had stayed up with Tallia to await further news. The other Potentials had also remained with them, for comfort. Tallia had tried hard to not upset them too much with the details of what occurred. But they knew the barebones. They knew Aris was shot but had healed incredibly quickly. That Maya's dad had been rescued from an unexpected kidnapping, and that Maya had now gone missing. Thomas told Tallia about a dream he'd had of Aris with a green light in his hand, but Tallia wasn't sure what that could mean.

They were delighted when the Seechers finally returned with Maya. Tallia took Sel and Pep to the medical room, as the other Seechers got out of their battle wear. Maya and Adam went to find somewhere quiet to be alone together, and Aris had taken himself off to the library to think things through. The rest of the Potentials had gone back to their dorm before Kat welcomed in an unexpected visitor who had arrived.

Maya and Adam were alone in a meditation room. Adam perched on a pillow as Maya wandered about.

"I can't believe Curative Analytical are behind all of this. How could I have been so naive? I just had no idea. Like, no idea. It was only when I realised that you were missing, that… You know, I never trusted any of them. I can't believe it. Right under my nose."

"How did they know about the Seechers?"

"I'm not sure. I downloaded some of their files to my hard drive, but that was in my bag, I don't know where that is now."

"Don't worry. You've been through so much, Maya. I'm so proud of you. Did you have any idea where they were taking you? Where they were going?"

"No. They never said."

"The Seechers will find them and put an end to this once and for all. I'm so happy I've got you back. The thought of losing you…I couldn't bear to thinking of it."

"Oh gosh, you too, dad. When I saw the CCTV footage of you, I was so worried you might…"

Adam stood up and hugged his daughter tightly as they shared their deep love of one another. "Dad, I'm really sorry for what I said to you, about wishing you dead." They hugged again.

Adam gently laughed at the irony of it. "It's not your fault, Maya."

Maya looked up at him. "But if I wasn't so ghastly to you that night and stormed out, you would never have gone looking for me, and none of this would have happened."

Adam held back the tears, as Maya threw her arms around him again.

"It's my fault, Tulip. For lying and keeping secrets from you. I shan't ever do that to you again. You were allowed to react, as you did. Don't ever think that any of this was your fault," Adam said as he stroked Maya's hair. "This is our chance at a second life, Maya. We have a lot to be grateful for."

Maya hugged him again even tighter.

Tallia entered the mastery-room. This was where the Seecher Masters had their meetings. It was a large room, with intricate ancient symbols carved into the stone walls. In the middle was a beautiful wooden round table.

Tallia squealed with surprised to find a familiar face that she'd not seen for a very long time, stand there in front of her.

"Marie. How lovely to see you," Tallia said.

"Tallia," replied Marie, her French accent bold and joyful.

The two women embraced. They were equal in height and complexion but differing in age. Marie was a good twenty years older than Tallia.

"It's good to see you looking so well," Tallia said as she turned to see who else was in the room.

Pep was at the head of the table. Kat sat at his left, and Sel at his right.

Marie was the Seecher Elder of the Paris Guild.

"Where's Adam?" Tallia asked as she and Marie took their seats.

"He's still talking with Maya. I'll discuss this with him tomorrow. I know it's been an extraordinarily long day, but it's important that you are aware of this as soon as possible," Pep said.

"Okay. Is this about the new threat?" Tallia asked.

"No," Sel said sternly.

Tallia raised her brow and sat down.

"As you know, Tallia, as soon as we became aware of Aris's unique Epsilon, I approached the other Guild Elders for their insights. Marie has uncovered something important," Pep announced.

"What did you find?" Tallia turned to Marie to ask.

"As soon as Pep described what was seen in the Mirror Sands to the Elders. I remembered hearing something about Epsilon in the blood before. I couldn't quite remember where I had read it. But I recalled it the other day, some references to some theories around the great Anaximander himself, made by Seechers in the seventeenth century."

"Anaximander?" Kat uttered, astounded. Kat knew, as all Seechers did, that the founding Seecher was born around 600BC. The Greek

Philosopher, Anaximander, was the one who discovered that the universe was born from Epsilon. He was the first to enter Nihilo and locate the original source of Epsilon. Throughout his lifetime, he made many discoveries into the Great Mystery, but none more important than the truth. That Epsilon lay dormant inside the pineal gland, or *third eye* of the human brain.

"Oui," Marie replied. "You see some Elders have previously proposed theories that Anaximander's Epsilon wasn't just confined to his pineal gland but was in fact distributed in his blood. It is well-known that a Key is never mentioned, and he was the first to enter Nihilo and return."

"We are all well aware of the great master's firsts triumphs. You're implying Aris has the same abilities as Anaximander?" Sel leant in.

"He healed his gunshot wound, using only his blood and his will. He'd watched me once whilst I partly healed him. I was shocked. I still am. An Aeon Seecher would take decades to achieve the level of healing he did. He's not even a Seecher yet! He is, without a doubt, extremely powerful." Tallia was concerned more than impressed. Seechers had reason to be wary of power and its corrupting influence.

"This is exactly why we must take this case very seriously indeed." Pep indicated for Marie to continue.

"Which led me to read something I had not read for many years but suddenly seemed… important. Relevant," Marie said as she looked directly at Pep.

"You are all familiar with the prophecies, made by the Great Porete?"

Everyone in the room was aware of the lives of Anaximander, Plato and Porete. They were referred to as the Great Lucasians. Each of them had mastered all Five Reflections. This was why it is speculated they were able to enter Nihilo and return. Gaining great wisdom from the subconscious world. The first two had founded most of the Seecher Covenant. Porete, however, had added a few chapters to the Covenant, but her most notable Seecher work were her prophecies. Said to have been informed by her experiences of Nihilo. It wasn't entirely uncommon for Seechers to enter Nihilo. What was rare was for them to return. The three Great Lucasians were the only recorded Seechers to enter Nihilo and return and were the only three Lucasians ever recorded doing so.

"I know the work of Porete is highly-regarded but reading through her prophecies is not something I've ever got around to doing," Kat replied. Sel nodded.

"I've read one or two. But they're cryptic and abstract," Tallia explained.

"I've read the originals, but it was a long time ago. I don't often put stock in Seecher prophecies, even ones from a Great Lucasian," Pep said.

"Well, unlike most other Elders. I have a passion for them. And when I recalled the similarities between your Potential and the First Great Lucasian, I knew I had to find this," Marie replied as she pulled out a file and opened it to a copy of a prophecy.

"This one is called the Last Lucasian Prophecy. And I feel you will find it interesting and hopefully informative," Marie said as she took the top piece of paper and passed it to Pep. He read it to himself.

"English translation for the others?" Pep asked.

"*Oui*, I am here to be helpful my friend," Marie replied. She then passed copies to the other three Seechers.

As Tallia took hers, she decided to read it aloud.

"For he is Lucasian, Pupil and Master.
He casts as Anaximander casts,
Aperion given shadow form.
Chaos consumes, Aeon and All,
For unlike the First, his Epsilon Torn.

For he is Lucasian, Here and Beyond.
Scales unbalanced, Oneiri controlled.
For his powers are Great and Unbound.
Take heed in this lesson, Origins Unknown,
He'll open the door to the Threat First told.

For he is Lucasian, Saviour and Death."

Tallia finished and paused. The other Seechers had stopped reading to listen to her. She looked over to Pep, who was genuinely disturbed by it.

"What does this even mean?" Tallia exclaimed.

"Details, I do not know. It is what it is. If he is a Lucasian, then there's a high chance this prophecy concerns your Potential," Marie said to a room full of contemplative faces.

"What are you thinking, Pep?" Sel asked.

"We don't know yet if Aris is a Lucasian. We will have to derive a test for it, but I don't want to treat him differently to the other Potentials whilst we are training. So, this will need great thought and secrecy. If it comes to pass, that he is the next Lucasian Seecher, how long it will take him to go from the activation to a Lucasian level of mastery, we have no idea. However, this prophecy is clearly concerning. But like many old prophecies, it's vague and unclear. We can't be sure it relates to Aris. But we can certainly approach his training with great caution," Pep said, sitting back down.

"Yes, you will need to take significant care in his training. We should all be prepared for what unleashing the first threat could mean. The Covenant is designed to protect against that threat above all else," Marie spoke, her voice quivering.

"The first threat? What is that reference to?" Kat asked.

"More vagueness, I assure you, Kat," Sel interjected.

"Sel, I agree, more vagueness. But many Seecher Elders have spent lifetimes contemplating the threat and what the consequences of unleashing it would be," Pep said, looking around the table.

"So, what is it?" Kat asked.

Marie stood before Pep could reply. They all turned to look at her as she cleared her throat. The fear that moments before had crept slightly into her words now drenched her voice.

"The end of the Seechers and our protection over *the balance*. The rise of the darkest kind of control in Nihilo. So strong it consumes and controls every mind alive. Robbing them from the inside, of their free will. Enslaving all, into a perpetual state of trepidation and fear."

———

Aris sat in an armchair. He'd been there for nearly two hours, ever since he'd returned to the guild. The first thing he did was to speak to his father on the phone. He had woken Peter up, but his dad said he was grateful for the money Aris had transferred him to pay off the bills. Aris didn't let him know the money had almost cost him his life. He didn't want to worry his father, so he tried to sound as normal as possible. He would go and see him first thing tomorrow.

Aris dipped in and out of reading the book he had started the other day. *The Seechers Covenant.* He was looking for answers.

There were two questions in the forefront of his mind: How did he create that energy wave in the Oneiri? And who is that woman?

He placed the book down as his stomach rumbled. He stood up to make his way out of the reading room to the kitchen when Maya crept in.

"Hey. You're still up," she said as her eyes met Aris's.

"Hey," Aris replied, throwing his arms around her in relief. "Are you okay?"

"Yeah. You?" Maya replied.

"A bit hungry." Aris nodded.

"How's your dad?" Aris indicated they sit down and talk.

"He's gone to sleep now, but he's good. Hey, guess what? He said I can train to be a Seecher, if I want to."

"That's great, Maya." Aris smiled.

"Thank you," Maya carried on.

"For what?"

"I heard you played a big part in my rescue. What would I do without you?"

"Ah, just a small part," Aris said. He was very unsure as to how he could describe what really happened. After all, Pep had told him that creating an energy wave in the Oneiri was impossible. So, why had it happened to him?

"When are you going to take the test?" Aris asked her.

"Tomorrow." Maya clapped.

"That's awesome, Maya," Aris looked to the floor.

"What's the matter?" Maya leant forward.

"We should go to bed, maybe talk in the morning," Aris said. "I'm zapped."

"Something's upsetting you. I can see it in your eyes," Maya said.

"You can tell me."

Aris thought for a moment. There was a lot on his mind, and if there was anyone he could tell his problems to, it was Maya.

"Okay. Yes, you're right. There is." Aris took in a deep breath and exhaled. Maya sat up straight.

"When I got out of the medical room, and Tallia told me you must have still been in the building and no one knew where you were, I got a little crazy with worry and needed some time on my own. I went to one of the bedrooms, and I ended up just staring at my reflection in one of the mirrors for ages." He stopped, the events playing out in his mind, trying to find a way of explaining without sounding too absurd.

"This might sound strange, but I swear it's true. Whilst I was looking at the mirror, I saw someone else. I saw a woman staring at me."

"A woman?" Maya interjected. "Who?"

"I don't know. I've never seen her before. I mean, I've never met her for real. But I am certain it was her who called out to me in the lecture hall when my dad fell ill. And she also told me not to go down the stairs in the hospital the night I was attacked. And she was also with me after I fell from the roof, into the water. She saved me. I know she did."

"Wow. Really?" Maya asked, her voice compassionate.

"I didn't see her, but I felt her carrying me out of the river."

"You're right, this does sound pretty strange. But no stranger than anything else that's happened in the last twenty-four hours. Did she say anything? What happened when you saw her in the mirror?"

"She told me to touch it with my blood. She told me the Oneiri was mine to control, to create. Then she vanished from the glass, and my reflection was gone, and all I could see was you handcuffed at the airfield," he replied, trying to explain it as coherently as possible.

"The Oneiri?" Maya asked, wanting to understand.

"It's the world in between our world and Nihilo, the subconscious world. It's the place we went through when we were in Curative Analytical. It's where all the energy from Nihilo filters into the Skia, into here, the Earth. It's the energy balance the Seechers protect. You know, when we went through the mirror?" Aris remembered.

"Right."

"But that's not all, Maya. I saw her again when we came to rescue you. The Seechers kept me from the fight, safe in the Oneiri. And she appeared to me again." Aris paused before continuing. He knew he needed to conceal some of the truths, only to share what wouldn't alarm her.

"As I stood watching the Seechers enter the airfield, I couldn't help but go, too, and see what was happening. I needed to know you were safe. I was there, but no one could see me." Maya smiled at the thought of Aris there.

"Right."

"She appeared and told me to… She said, I had to let go. I asked her who she was. She simply replied, *To find me is to know yourself.*"

"What the fuck. That doesn't make sense. To find her is to know yourself? What?!"

"As soon as she finished speaking, she rose off the ground. It was like she floated. No, it was like she was being dragged away. She rose, high into the sky, and I lost sight of her," he said, locking eyes with Maya's.

Maya got up from the chair and absently spoke to herself, "Strange, so strange. I wonder who she is? What did she mean? Aris, this is amazing. Even for Seechers, this sounds pretty extraordinary. Have you told anyone else?"

"No! I wouldn't know how to begin. Like you said, it sounds very different from anything else I've heard about the Seechers. I just don't know," Aris threw his hands in the air.

"Let's get some food and go to sleep. We can think about it tomorrow. You know, I'm always here for you," she smiled at Aris. He mirrored her joy.

"I'm so happy you're okay," Aris stood up next to Maya.

Maya blushed and took his hand. "Come on. Food and sleep." But before they left the room, Maya turned to him and asked, "Who do you think she is?"

"I don't know. But there's one thing I feel certain about."

"What?" Maya paused.

"She's from Nihilo. And I want to somehow…" Aris paused.

"Somehow, what?"

"Go there." Aris whispered with a glint in his eyes.

Glossary of Terms

Activation Tank
A highly secure tank, in a Seecher guild, that is very sophisticated, allowing a Potential Seecher to extract the Epsilon from their pineal gland and place it into a Seecher Key. It's an extremely special room that bridges the dimensions between Nihilo and dreams. The process does not damage the head or brain in anyway, although the instructions are complicated and it's a dangerous task to undertake.

Aeon
The Reflection of life. This reflection is in and gives life, to all living things.

Alcaios Warrior
Alcaios Warrior Seechers are the soldiers of the Seecher world. They have received specific and advanced combat training, in the Alcaios headquarters, hidden deep within the mountains of Tibet.

Epsilac
Epsilac is the term used to describe 'dead' Epsilon. If Epsilon is extracted using unconventional and crude methods, the consciousness of the Epsilon is not retained, leaving it a glowing dandelion yellow. Epsilac is not as potent as Epsilon. Epsilac was first discovered and used by the Tauredunum Raiders.

Epsilon
Epsilon is a fluorescent blue liquid. This substance resides within the minds of all beings. The amount of Epsilon within a person's brain varies. Having more Epsilon in the brain indicates that someone is a Potential and has the possibility of becoming a Seecher.

Five Reflections

There are Five Reflections that enclose our reality that give form, depth, duration, thought and breath to our universe. These are also referred to as the Great Mystery. The Reflections are: Time. Space. Matter. Life. Mind.

Guild Elder

A Guild Elder is the Seecher who has been selected to be the responsible head of one of the thirty three Seecher guilds. Guild Elders are the commander and the person responsible for the daily running and prosperity of their respective guild.

Hyle

The Reflection of matter. This reflection gives form to all matter in the universe.

Karios

The Reflection of time. This reflection gives duration; circular and linear, to our world.

Keno

The Reflection of space. This reflection gives depth and volume to the universe and fills all the spaces that are in between things.

Kinesis

Is a Seecher's command in the Oneiri, to move energy waves with direction from their thought, projected through the palms of their hands.

Lucasian

A Lacasian Seecher is one who has mastered all Five Reflections and can manipulate all the Reflections simultaneously. It is a rare accomplishment and has only been witnessed three times in Seecher history.

Nihilo

Nihilo is described as the Subconscious World where all life and consciousness stems from. It is the immense world beyond our own, an Eden like utopian nirvana that all living things are connected too, through the subconscious.

Nous

The Reflection of mind. This reflection is in and gives consciousness, to sentient thought.

Oneiri

The Oneiri is a world embedded within the Reflections, like a 4th dimensional world, that lies between our world and Nihilo. In the Oneiri, Seechers can see the energy balance that comes from Nihilo that affects our world, the Skia.

Potential

A Potential is an individual who has the prospect to undergo the Trials and the Activation Tank to become a Seecher. They posses greater quantities of Epsilon in their brain than the average person.

Seecher

A Seecher is an individual who was once a Potential who has faced and passed the Seecher trails and has undergone the transformation into a Seecher in an activation tank. They own a Seecher Key. and have the ability to manipulate the Reflections. All Seechers make an oath to uphold the principles of the Covenant.

Seecher Key

A Seecher Key is the most sacred object for a Seecher. It is obtained in an activation tank and contains a Seecher's own Epsilon. When in possession of a Seecher Key, a Seecher can manipulate the Reflections around them at will, through conscious thought and skill. A Seecher Key is a miniature Klein bottle, fluorescent blue in appearance.

Seecher Trials

The Seecher trials are an ancient set of puzzles and exercises designed to enhance a Potential's understanding and skills to be able to experience the great mysteries of the Reflections and prepare for the activation tank.

Skia

The Skia is what the Seechers refer to as our world. Though it is not as we have imagined it to be and it is constructed out of the Five Reflections, that come from Nihilo.

Spilio

Is a Seecher's command in the Oneiri to reveal a vision of Nihilo. The command is said and the thought and will is projected through the palms of their hands.

Subconscious Institute (S.I.)

The Subconscious Institute are an organization that stem from a top-secret branch from the Ministry of Defence. They fractioned off and created their own private company, as they discovered Tauredunum technology and a means to extract Epsilac. Their departmental structure allows them to successfully keep secrets, even between members of their own staff.

Tauredunum

The Tauredunum Raiders were a group of powerful men who formed an organization to steal Epsilon from the Seechers and used it as a source of power to control and conquer. They have long since died out, but their incredibly advanced technology was rediscovered in more recent years, by the S.I.

Tyche

Is a Seecher's command in the Oneiri to reveal and to hide the energy waves .The command is said and the thought and will is projected through the palms of their hands.

Special thanks to Christopher Snell for believing in us. Also, to Olive Maddison, Suzanne Kavanagh, Heather Parsons, Nic Marshall and Ben Lloyd for your invaluable notes and feedback. Thank you to Gerry Kavanagh for being a pillar of support. Thank you to Garry Maddison, Judah Kavanagh, and Wolfie. To both of our families and friends. And to the amazing 43 backers from our Kickstarter, who made this possible. From the bottom of our hearts, thank you.

Printed in Great Britain
by Amazon

61640057R00116